NEAPOLITAN CHRONICLES

ANNA MARIA ORTESE

Translated by
ANN GOLDSTEIN
and
JENNY McPHEE

NEW VESSEL PRESS
NEW YORK

www.newvesselpress.com

New Vessel Press

First published in Italian in 1953 by Giulio Einaudi, Turin, as *Il mare non bagna Napoli*
Copyright © 1994 Adelphi Edizioni, Milan
Translation Copyright © 2018 Ann Goldstein and Jenny McPhee

All rights reserved. Except for brief passages quoted in a newspaper, magazine, radio, television, or website review, no part of this book may be reproduced in any form or by any means, electronic or mechanical, including photocopying and recording, or by any information storage and retrieval system, without permission in writing from the Publisher.

Questo libro è stato tradotto grazie ad un contributo alla traduzione assegnato dal Ministero degli Affari esteri e della Cooperazione Internazionale Italiano.

This book has been translated thanks to a grant by the
Italian Ministry of Foreign Affairs and International Cooperation.

Library of Congress Cataloging-in-Publication Data
Ortese, Anna Maria
[Il mare non bagna Napoli. English]
Neapolitan Chronicles/ Anna Maria Ortese; translation by Ann Goldstein
and Jenny McPhee.
p. cm.
ISBN 978-1-939931-51-1

Library of Congress Control Number 2017949071
I. Italy—Fiction and Nonfiction

TABLE OF CONTENTS

TRANSLATORS' INTRODUCTION   I

PREFACE   9
The "Sea" as Disorientation

A PAIR OF EYEGLASSES   13

FAMILY INTERIOR   35

THE GOLD OF FORCELLA   63

THE INVOLUNTARY CITY   73

THE SILENCE OF REASON   99
    Evening Descends Upon the Hills   *101*
    The Story of Luigi the Bureaucrat   *115*
    Chiaia: Dead and Restless   *131*
    Worker's Identification Card No. 200774   *147*
    Literal Translation: "What is the meaning of this night?"   *161*
    The Boy from Monte di Dio   *173*

AFTERWORD   189
The Gray Jackets of Monte di Dio

TRANSLATORS' INTRODUCTION

I n January, 1933, Anna Maria Ortese's brother Emanuele Carlo, a sailor in the Italian Navy, died during a maneuver off the island of Martinique. "The effect of this news on the household was at first a kind of inferno, but then a strange silence," Ortese wrote many years later. "It's like an amputation: a part of the soul is gone forever. And the soul reacts by ceasing to listen to any noise or sound or voice of the surrounding nature or of its own life ... That silence, at least for me, who was always alone ... lasted several months, and I couldn't see any way out. Finally, one day—rather, one morning—I suddenly thought that, since I was dying from it, I could at least describe it." The result was a poem, "Manuele," published in the review *L'Italia Letteraria*, in September of the same year. Ortese went on to say, "My life, from that day, changed radically, because now I had a means through which to express myself." The editor of the review, Corrado Pavolini, continued to publish her poems, among those of such writers as Salvatore Quasimodo, Giuseppe Ungaretti, and Umberto Saba, and suggested that she also try writing stories.

Ortese was born in Rome in 1914, one of six children, into a peripatetic and economically struggling family. Her father was a government employee and was often transferred; the family lived all over Italy and also, for three years, in Libya. In 1928 they settled in Naples, her mother's native city. Ortese had little formal education, but, with Pavolini's encouragement, she continued to write stories, publishing them in *L'Italia Letteraria* and other reviews, many of them under the pseudonym Franca Nicosi, in order to avoid her family's disapproval. The new editor of *L'Italia Letteraria*, Massimo Bontempelli, brought her work to the attention of the publisher Valentino Bompiani, and, in 1937, he brought out a collection of her stories, *Angelici Dolori* (The Sorrows of Angels). When the war came, the family was displaced many times, but in 1945 returned, finally, to Naples. Ortese had begun working as a journalist, while continuing to write stories; in 1950 she published a second collection of stories, and in 1953 *Neapolitan Chronicles*, a book that includes both fiction and journalism.

Neapolitan Chronicles presented a Naples "shattered by war," in which suffering and corruption were widespread and very real. Ortese's bleak picture takes in not only the struggling masses of the poor but bourgeois, aristocratic, and intellectual Naples as well. Of the five chapters, three are fiction and two are journalistic accounts arising from intensive research and, at times, intrepid reportage. The first story, "A Pair of Eyeglasses," set mainly among the residents surrounding a squalid courtyard in one of the city's densely packed neighborhoods, is told essentially from the point of view of a child who is nearly blind, and contrasts the child's blurred view of her surroundings, and her desire to see clearly, with the brutal, ugly world she will see when she gets her glasses. Vision—seeing, observing, taking in—is both a reality and a stark metaphor for Ortese throughout *Neapolitan Chronicles*. In "Family Interior," Anastasia, a hardworking shop owner who has been supporting her mother and siblings for years for the first time in her life allows herself to see the grasping, selfish nature of her family, and to imagine something different from her life of "house and shop, shop and house," but it's a vision that can't be sustained: when her mother calls, she can only say "I'm coming." "The Gold of Forcella" returns to the crowded, destitute Naples of "A Pair of Eyeglasses," and the desperation of the women who have come to the charity pawnshop of the Bank of Naples to try to get a few thousand lire for some small, precious possession.

"The Involuntary City" is a portrait of the inhabitants of Granili III and IV, a notorious eighteenth-century building intended to be temporary housing for the homeless and the displaced after the war. The essay was first published in the review *Il Mondo*, in two parts, the second of which was titled "The Horror of Living." The narrator tries to convey the horror first by a recitation of data about the "structure and population" of the place, but immediately realizes that this is insufficient and goes on to describe entering the "almost absolute" darkness of the ground-floor corridor, making her way through the entire building in order to record the grim human details of life there. Elena Ferrante, long before the publication of *The Neapolitan Novels*, said of "The Involuntary City" that if she were to write about Naples she would want to explore the direction indicated by Ortese's account: a story of "small, wretched acts of violence, an abyss of voices and events, tiny terrible gestures."

The last chapter, the long chronicle "The Silence of Reason," describes a journey to postwar Naples in which Ortese visits several of the writers and editors who had been her colleagues at the avant-garde literary and cultural magazine *Sud*, published between 1945 and 1947. In this account, she wanders around

Naples, both seeing and recalling people and places, and finds that her former colleagues have, essentially, betrayed their youthful ideals, becoming complacent and bourgeois.

The book brought Ortese attention ("I suddenly found myself almost famous") and won the Premio Viareggio, an important literary prize, but its reception was mixed. On the one hand, its depiction of a harsh, ugly, impoverished, and corrupt postwar Naples (and postwar Italy) was seen as something new and necessary; on the other the book was viewed as "anti-Naples," an indictment of the city, particularly by the young intellectuals described in the final chapter as having compromised their beliefs, who saw it as both a personal betrayal and a betrayal of the city. As a result of the book's "condemnation," she writes, she "said goodbye to my city—a decision that subsequently became permanent." Indeed, in the fifty years following the book's publication, she returned to Naples only once.

Neapolitan Chronicles sold well, but Ortese complained that she got nothing from it, having already used up her advance: and this was to be her situation for most of her life. Although she worked constantly, publishing journalism, stories, and eleven novels, she always struggled to have enough money to live, and sometimes had to rely on the financial help of friends. In 1986, the publishing house Adelphi, headed by Roberto Calasso, began reprinting Ortese's earlier works and publishing her new ones. It was a fortunate development—"They believed in my books [and] published them with respect"—which, finally, brought her acclaim in Italy. She had rarely stayed long in one place, living variously in Milan, Rome, Venice, and Florence, but this, too, changed in her final years, when, with a pension from the government, she was able to settle with her sister in Rapallo. She died there in 1998.

In both her fiction and her reporting, Ortese's style is an arresting mixture of realist detail and an almost surreal tone, with a strong underlying moral and social sensibility. In a preface to a new edition of *Neapolitan Chronicles*, brought out by Adelphi in 1994, Ortese said of the writing that it "tends toward the high-pitched, encroaches on the hallucinatory, and at almost every point on the page displays, even in its precision, something of the 'too much.'" This may be particularly true in "The Involuntary City," in which the smells, sounds, and sights of the place possess these very qualities. Near a mattress on the floor in one room, the narrator says, "there were some crusts of bread, and amid these, barely moving, like dust balls, three long sewer rats were gnawing on the bread." The voice of the woman who lives in the room "was so normal, in its weary disgust, and the scene so tranquil, and those three animals appeared so sure of being able to gnaw on those crusts of bread, that I had the impression that I was dreaming."

Similarly in a talk (never delivered) written in 1980 she says: "If I had to define everything that surrounds me: things, in their infinity, or my feeling about things, and this for half a century, I could not use any other word than this: strangeness. And the desire—rather, the painful urgency—to render, in my writing, the feeling of strangeness." In all the stories of *Neapolitan Chronicles*, people and places that should be familiar are not; in the 1994 preface she talks about her own "disorientation" from reality. This disorientation is literal in "A Pair of Eyeglasses," when the nearly blind Eugenia finally puts on her eyeglasses: "Her legs were trembling, her head was spinning, and she no longer felt any joy ... Suddenly the balconies began to multiply, two thousand, a hundred thousand; the carts piled with vegetables were falling on her; the voices filling the air, the cries, the lashes, struck her head as if she were ill." And strangeness, or estrangement, is precisely one of the themes of "The Silence of Reason," in which the narrator arrives at the house of one of her former colleagues and, when no one answers the bell, stands staring through the glass panes of a door into a dark room whose features only gradually, and painstakingly, come into focus, recognizable but different and, ultimately, alienating.

Although no writer can be said to be "easy" to translate, Ortese's style presents some particular difficulties. Her sentences can be convoluted and complex. The language can sometimes seem repetitive and, as she says, "high-pitched" and "feverish," qualities that can be off-putting. The metaphors are sometimes bewildering. There are many topographical references to the city of Naples that we didn't try to explain, but we have provided some basic information about the writers mentioned in the final chapter.

   Neapolitan Chronicles was first published by Einaudi, in the Gettoni series,* and was originally titled *Il mare non bagna Napoli,* or *Naples Is Not Bathed by the Sea.* That title, chosen by Ortese's editors at Einaudi, Italo Calvino and Elio Vittorini, comes from a line in the story "The Gold of Forcella," and was intended to signify that although the sea is one of the most beautiful and

---

* The Gettoni series, initiated by Elio Vittorini, came out between 1951 and 1958, and included fifty-eight titles, eight by non-Italians. *Gettone* means "token" in Italian, and up until 2001 a metal token was commonly used in Italy for public telephones, and also for arcade games. The idea was that the books in the series would be affordable and would increase communication and a sense of playfulness through literature by reaching a wide and younger audience. Among the authors published in the Gettoni series were, besides Ortese, Italo Calvino, Lalla Romano, Marguerite Duras, Beppe Fenoglio, Nelson Algren, Leonardo Sciascia, Dylan Thomas, Mario Rigoni Stern, and Jorge Luis Borges.

animating features of Naples, it offers the suffering city no solace or relief. *Neapolitan Chronicles* is another title that Ortese was considering, and it seemed to us a more apt description of the book's contents. The text is based on the 1994 Adelphi edition, and includes the preface and an afterword that was also part of that edition.

For both of us, this was the first experience of co-translating a work of literature. Rather than each being responsible for a number of stories, we divided them, arbitrarily, for a first draft, and then traded. We continued sending the stories back and forth, with discussions in notes, and sometimes in person, until the manuscript was ready.

The role of the translator in a work of literature is much discussed and debated. Some believe that at best the translator is invisible; others say that he or she is, inevitably, a traitor to the original text. Still others claim that the translator is the creator of an entirely new work of literature. As for us, individually, we fall respectively at different places along that continuum.

Whatever the role of the translator, the work of the translator, like the work of the writer, is apparently a solitary endeavor. Yet translating and writing are profoundly collaborative acts across time and texts, involving an ongoing, cacophonous conversation among writers and translators.

We have not only been part of this greater conversation; we have also carried on a conversation with each other for more than twenty years. The decision to challenge and explore our own process as translators by collaborating on a text in this way and seeing what came of it was interesting, informative, surprising, and above all, delightful. Having another person's ideas and point of view during the practice of translating was both intriguing and invaluable. By the end of our project, we could not have said who had written a given sentence or come up with a particular word. We had in essence merged into yet another translator, who was at once invisible, and at the same time, had a style all her own.

Ann Goldstein and Jenny McPhee

PREFACE

The "Sea" as Disorientation

⌒⌒⌒⌒

Neapolitan Chronicles first appeared in Einaudi's Gettoni series, with an introduction by Elio Vittorini. It was 1953. Italy had come out of the war full of hope, and everything was up for discussion. Owing to its subject matter, my book was also part of the discussion: unfortunately, it was judged to be "anti-Naples." As a result of this condemnation, I said goodbye to my city—a decision that subsequently became permanent. In the nearly forty years that have passed since then, I have returned to Naples only once, fleetingly, for just a few hours.

At a distance of four decades, and on the occasion of a new edition of the book, I now wonder if *Chronicles* really was "anti-Naples," and what, if anything, I did wrong in the writing of it, and how the book should be read today.

The writing seems to me to be the best place to start, although many may find it difficult to understand how *writing* can be the unique key to the reading of a text, and provide hints about its possible truth.

Well, the writing in *Chronicles* has something of the exalted and the feverish; it tends toward the high-pitched, encroaches on the hallucinatory, and at almost every point on the page displays, even in its precision, something of the too much. Evident in it are all the signs of an authentic neurosis.

That neurosis was mine. It would take too long and would be impossible to say where its origin is; but since it is right to point out an origin, even if confused, I will point out the one that is most incredible and also least suited to the indulgence of the political types (who were, I believe, my only critics and detractors). That origin, and the source of my neurosis, had a single name: metaphysics.

For a very long time, I hated with all my might, almost without knowing it, so-called *reality*: that mechanism of things that arise in time and are destroyed by time. This reality for me was incomprehensible and ghastly.

Rejection of that *reality* was the secret of my first book, published in 1937 by Bompiani, and mocked by the champions of the "real" at the time.

I would add that my personal experience of the war (terror everywhere and four years of flight) had brought my irritation with the real to the limit. And the disorientation I suffered from was by now so acute—and was also nearly unmentionable, since it had no validation in the common experience—that it required an extraordinary occasion in order to reveal itself.

That occasion was my encounter with postwar Naples.

Seeing Naples again and grieving for it was not enough. Someone had written that this Naples reflected a universal condition of being torn apart. I agreed, but not to the (implicit) acceptance of this wretched state of affairs. And if the lacerated condition originated in the infinite blindness of life, then it was this life, and its obscure nature, that I invoked.

I myself was shut up in that dark seed of life, and thus—

through my neurosis—I was crying out. That is, I cried out.

Naples was shattered by the war, and the suffering and the corruption were very real. But Naples was a limitless city, and it also enjoyed the infinite resources of its natural beauty, the vitality of its roots. I, instead, had no roots, or was about to lose the ones that were left, and I attributed to this beautiful city the *disorientation* that was primarily mine. The horror that I attributed to the city was my own weakness.

I have long regretted it, and have tried many times to clarify how well I understand the discomfort of a typical Italian reader who wasn't told—nor did I myself know, nor could I say it— that *Chronicles* was only a screen, though not entirely illusory, on which to project the painful disorientation, the "dark suffering of life," as it came to be called, of the person who had written the book.

The rather sad (or only unusual?) fact remains that the Naples that was offended (was it really offended or only a little indifferent?) and the person accused of having invented a terrible neurosis for the city were never to meet again: *almost as if nothing had happened.*

And for me, it wasn't like that.

April 1994

A PAIR OF EYEGLASSES

"As long as there's the sun … the sun!" the voice of Don Peppino Quaglia crooned softly near the doorway of the low, dark, basement apartment. "Leave it to God," answered the humble and faintly cheerful voice of his wife, Rosa, from inside; she was in bed, moaning in pain from arthritis, complicated by heart disease, and, addressing her sister-in-law, who was in the bathroom, she added: "You know what I'll do, Nunziata? Later I'll get up and take the clothes out of the water."

"Do as you like, to me it seems real madness," replied the curt, sad voice of Nunziata from that den. "With the pain you have, one more day in bed wouldn't hurt you!" A silence. "We've got to put out some more poison, I found a cockroach in my sleeve this morning."

From the cot at the back of the room, which was really a cave, with a low vault of dangling spiderwebs, rose the small, calm voice of Eugenia:

"Mamma, today I'm putting on the eyeglasses."

There was a kind of secret joy in the modest voice of the child, Don Peppino's third-born. (The first two, Carmela and Luisella, were with the nuns, and would soon take the veil, hav-

13

ing been persuaded that this life is a punishment; and the two little ones, Pasqualino and Teresella, were still snoring, as they slept feet to head, in their mother's bed.)

"Yes, and no doubt you'll break them right away," the voice of her aunt, still irritated, insisted, from behind the door of the little room. She made everyone suffer for the disappointments of her life, first among them that she wasn't married and had to be subject, as she told it, to the charity of her sister-in-law, although she didn't fail to add that she dedicated this humiliation to God. She had something of her own set aside, however, and wasn't a bad person, since she had offered to have glasses made for Eugenia when at home they had realized that the child couldn't see. "With what they cost! A grand total of a good eight thousand lire!" she added. Then they heard the water running in the basin. She was washing her face, squeezing her eyes, which were full of soap, and Eugenia gave up answering.

Besides, she was too, too pleased.

A week earlier, she had gone with her aunt to an optician on Via Roma. There, in that elegant shop, full of polished tables and with a marvelous green reflection pouring in through a blind, the doctor had measured her sight, making her read many times, through certain lenses that he kept changing, entire columns of letters of the alphabet, printed on a card, some as big as boxes, others as tiny as pins. "This poor girl is almost blind," he had said then, with a kind of pity, to her aunt, "she should no longer be deprived of lenses." And right away, while Eugenia, sitting on a stool, waited anxiously, he had placed over her eyes another pair of lenses, with a white metal frame, and had said: "Now look into the street." Eugenia stood up, her legs trembling with emotion, and was unable to suppress a little cry of joy. On the sidewalk, so many well-dressed people were passing, slightly smaller than normal but very distinct: ladies in silk dresses with powdered faces, young men with long hair and bright-colored sweaters, white-bearded old men with pink hands resting on silver-handled canes; and, in the middle of the street, some beautiful automobiles that looked like toys, their bodies painted red or teal, all shiny; green trolleys as big as houses, with their windows lowered, and behind the windows so many people in elegant clothes. Across the street, on the opposite sidewalk, were beautiful shops, with windows like mirrors, full of things so fine they elicited a kind of longing; some shop boys in black aprons were polishing the windows from the street. At a café with red and yellow tables, some golden-haired girls were sitting outside, legs crossed. They laughed and drank from big colored glasses. Above the café, because it was already spring, the balcony windows were open and embroidered curtains swayed, and behind the curtains were fragments of blue and gilded paintings, and heavy, sparkling chandeliers of gold and crystal, like baskets of artificial fruit. A marvel. Transported by all that splendor, she hadn't followed the conversation between the doctor and her aunt. Her aunt, in the brown dress she wore to Mass, and standing back from the glass counter with a timidity unnatural to her, now broached the question of the cost: "Doctor, please, give us a good price … we're poor folk …" and when she heard "eight thousand lire" she nearly fainted.

"Two lenses! What are you saying! Jesus Mary!"

"Look, ignorant people …" the doctor answered, replacing the other lenses after polishing them with the glove, "don't calculate anything. And when you give the child two lenses, you'll be able to tell me if she sees better. She takes nine diopters on one side, and ten on the other, if you want to know … she's almost blind."

While the doctor was writing the child's first and last name—"Eugenia Quaglia, Vicolo della Cupa at Santa Maria in Portico"—Nunziata had gone over to Eugenia, who, standing in the doorway of the shop and holding up the glasses in her small, sweaty hands, was not at all tired of gazing through them: "Look, look, my dear! See what your consolation costs! Eight thousand lire, did you hear? A grand total of a good eight thousand lire!" She was almost suffocating. Eugenia had turned all red, not so much because of the rebuke as because the young woman at the cash register was looking at her, while her aunt was making that observation, which declared the family's poverty. She took off the glasses.

"But how is it, so young and already so nearsighted?" the young woman had asked Nunziata, while she signed the receipt for the deposit. "And so shabby, too!" she added.

"Young lady, in our house we all have good eyes, this is a misfortune that came upon us … along with the rest. God rubs salt in the wound."

"Come back in eight days," the doctor had said. "I'll have them for you."

Leaving, Eugenia had tripped on the step.

"Thank you, Aunt Nunzia," she had said after a while. "I'm always rude to you. I talk back to you, and you are so kind, buying me eyeglasses."

Her voice trembled.

"My child, it's better not to see the world than to see it," Nunziata had answered with sudden melancholy.

Eugenia hadn't answered her that time, either. Aunt Nunzia was often so strange, she wept and shouted for no good reason, she said so many bad words, and yet she went to Mass regularly, she was a good Christian, and when it came to helping someone in trouble she always volunteered, wholeheartedly. One didn't have to watch over her.

Since that day, Eugenia had lived in a kind of rapture, waiting for the blessed glasses that would allow her to see all people and things in their tiny details. Until then, she had been wrapped in a fog: the room where she lived, the courtyard always full of hanging laundry, the alley overflowing with colors and cries, everything for her was covered by a thin veil: she knew well only the faces of her family, especially her mother and her siblings, because often she slept with them, and sometimes she woke at night and, in the light of the oil lamp, looked at them. Her mother slept with her mouth open, her broken yellow teeth visible; her brother and sister, Pasqualino and Teresella, were always dirty and snot-nosed and covered with boils: when they slept, they made a strange noise, as if they had wild animals inside them. Sometimes Eugenia surprised herself by staring at them, without understanding, however, what she was thinking. She had a confused feeling that beyond that room always full of wet laundry, with broken chairs and a stinking toilet, there was light, sounds, beautiful things, and in that moment when she had put on the glasses she had had a true revelation: the world outside was beautiful, very beautiful.

"Marchesa, my respects."

That was the voice of her father. Covered by a ragged shirt, his back, which until that moment had been framed by the doorway of the basement apartment, could no longer be seen. The voice of the marchesa, a placid and indifferent voice, now said:

"You must do me a favor, Don Peppino."

"At your service ... your wish is my command."

Silently, Eugenia slid out of bed, put on her dress, and, still barefoot, went to the door. The pure and marvelous early morning sun, entering the ugly courtyard through a crack between the buildings, greeted her, lit up her little old lady's face, her stubbly, disheveled hair, her rough, hard little hands, with their long, dirty nails. Oh, if only at that moment she could have had the eyeglasses! The marchesa was there, in her black silk dress with its white lace neckpiece. Her imposing yet benign appearance enchanted Eugenia, along with her bejeweled white hands; but she couldn't see her face very well—it was a whitish oval patch. Above it, some purple feathers quivered.

"Listen, you have to redo the child's mattress. Can you come up around ten-thirty?"

"With all my heart, but I'm only available in the afternoon, Signora Marchesa."

"No, Don Peppino, it has to be this morning. In the afternoon people are coming. Set yourself up on the terrace and work. Don't play hard to get ... do me this favor ... Now it's time for Mass. At ten-thirty, call me."

And without waiting for an answer, she left, astutely avoiding a trickle of yellow water that was dripping down from a terrace and had made a puddle on the ground.

"Papa," said Eugenia, following her father, as he went back inside, "how good the marchesa is! She treats you like a gentleman. God should reward her for it."

"A good Christian, that one is," Don Peppino answered, with a meaning completely different from what might have been understood. With the excuse that she was the owner of the house, the Marchesa D'Avanzo constantly had the people in the courtyard serving her: to Don Peppino, she gave a wretched sum for the mattresses; and Rosa was always available for the big sheets; even if her bones were burning she had to get up to serve the marchesa. It's true that the marchesa had placed her daughters in the convent, and so had saved two souls from the dangers of this world, which for the poor are many, but for that basement space, where everyone was sick, she collected three thousand lire, not one less. "The heart is there, it's the money that's lacking," she loved to repeat, with a certain imperturbability. "Today, dear Don Peppino, you are the nobility, who have no worries ... Thank ... thank Providence, which has put you in such a condition ... which wanted to save you." Donna Rosa had a kind of adoration for the marchesa, for her religious sentiments; when they saw each other, they always talked about the afterlife. The marchesa didn't much believe in it, but she didn't say so, and urged that mother of the family to be patient and to hope.

From the bed, Donna Rosa asked, a little worried: "Did you talk to her?"

"She wants me to redo the mattress for her grandson," said Don Peppino, in annoyance. He brought out the hot plate to warm up some coffee, a gift of the nuns, and went back inside to fetch water in a small pot. "I won't do it for less than five hundred," he said.

"It's a fair price."

"And then who will go and pick up Eugenia's glasses?" Aunt Nunzia asked, coming out of the bathroom. Over her nightgown, she wore a torn skirt, and on her feet slippers. Her bony shoulders emerged from the nightgown, gray as stones. She was drying her face with a napkin. "I can't go, and Rosa is ill."

Without anyone noticing, Eugenia's large, almost blind eyes

filled with tears. Now maybe another day would pass without her eyeglasses. She went up to her mother's bed, and in a pitiful manner, flung her arms and forehead on the blanket. Donna Rosa stretched out a hand to caress her.

"I'll go, Nunzia, don't get worked up … In fact, going out will do me good."

"Mamma …"

Eugenia kissed her hand.

Around eight there was a great commotion in the courtyard. At that moment Rosa had come out of the doorway: a tall, lanky figure, in a short, stained black coat, without shoulder pads, that exposed her legs, like wooden sticks. Under her arm, she carried a shopping bag for the bread she would buy on her way home from the optician. Don Peppino was pushing the water out of the middle of the courtyard with a long-handled broom, a vain task because the tub was continually leaking, like an open vein. In it were the clothes of two families: the Greborio sisters, on the second floor, and the wife of Cavaliere Amodio, who had given birth two days earlier. The Greborios' servant, Lina Tarallo, was beating the carpets on a balcony, making a terrible ruckus. The dust, mixed with garbage, descended gradually like a cloud on those poor people, but no one paid attention. Sharp screams and cries of complaint could be heard from the basement where Aunt Nunzia was calling on all the saints as witnesses to confirm that she was unfortunate, and the cause of all this was Pasqualino, who wept and shouted like a condemned man because he wanted to go with his mamma. "Look at him, this scoundrel," cried Aunt Nunzia. "*Madonna bella*, do me a favor, let me die, but immediately, if you're there, since in this life only thieves and whores thrive." Teresella, born the year the king went away and so younger than her brother, was sitting in the doorway, smiling, and every so often she licked a crust of bread she had found under a chair.

Eugenia was sitting on the step of another basement room, where Mariuccia the porter lived, looking at a section of a children's comic, with lots of bright-colored figures, which had fallen from the fourth floor. She held it right up to her face, because otherwise she couldn't read the words. There was a small blue river in a vast meadow and a red boat going … going … who knows where. It was written in proper Italian, and so she didn't understand much, but every so often, for no reason, she laughed.

"So, today you put on your glasses?" said Mariuccia, looking out from behind her. Everyone in the courtyard knew, partly because Eugenia hadn't resisted the temptation to talk about it, and partly because Aunt Nunzia had found it necessary to let it be understood that in that family she was spending her own … and well, in short …

"Your aunt got them for you, eh?" Mariuccia added, smiling good-humoredly. She was a small woman, almost a dwarf, with a face like a man's, covered with whiskers. At the moment she was combing her long black hair, which came to her knees: one of the few things that attested to her being a woman. She was combing it slowly, smiling with her sly but kind little mouse eyes.

"Mamma went to get them on Via Roma," said Eugenia with a look of gratitude. "We paid a grand total of a good eight thousand lire, you know? Really … my aunt is …" she was about to add "truly a good person," when Aunt Nunzia, looking out of the basement room, called angrily: "Eugenia!"

"Here I am, Aunt!" and she scampered away like a dog.

Behind their aunt, Pasqualino, all red-faced and bewildered, with a terrible expression somewhere between disdain and surprise, was waiting.

"Go and buy two candies for three lire each, from Don Vincenzo at the tobacco store. Come back immediately!"

"Yes, Aunt."

She clutched the money in her fist, paying no more attention to the comic, and hurried out of the courtyard.

By a true miracle she avoided a towering vegetable cart drawn by two horses, which was coming toward her right outside the main entrance. The carter, with his whip unsheathed, seemed to be singing, and from his mouth came these words: "Lovely … Fresh," drawn out and full of sweetness, like a love song. When the cart was behind her, Eugenia, raising her protruding eyes, basked in that warm blue glow that was the sky, and heard the great hubbub all around her, without, however, seeing it clearly. Carts, one behind the other, big trucks with Americans dressed in yellow hanging out the windows, bicycles that seemed to be tumbling over. High up, all the balconies were cluttered with flower crates, and over the railings, like flags or saddle blankets, hung yellow and red quilts, ragged blue children's clothes, sheets, pillows, and mattresses exposed to the air, while at the end of the alley ropes uncoiled, lowering baskets to pick up the vegetables or fish offered by peddlers. Although the sun touched only the highest balconies (the street a crack in the disorderly mass of buildings) and the rest was only shadow and garbage, one could sense, behind it, the enormous celebration of spring. And even Eugenia, so small and pale, bound like a mouse to the mud of her courtyard, began to breathe rapidly, as if that air, that celebration, and all that blue suspended over the neighborhood of the poor were also hers. The yellow basket of the Amodios' maid, Rosaria Buonincontri, grazed her as she went into the tobacco shop. Rosaria was a fat woman in black, with white legs and a flushed, placid face.

"Tell your mamma if she can come upstairs a moment today, Signora Amodio needs her to deliver a message."

Eugenia recognized her by her voice. "She's not here now. She went to Via Roma to get my glasses."

"I should wear them, too, but my boyfriend doesn't want me to."

Eugenia didn't grasp the meaning of that prohibition. She answered only, ingenuously: "They cost a great amount; you have to take very good care of them."

They entered Don Vincenzo's hole-in-the-wall together. There was a crowd. Eugenia kept being pushed back. "Go on … you really are blind," observed the Amodios' maid, with a kind smile.

"But now Aunt Nunzia's gotten you some eyeglasses," Don Vincenzo, who had heard her, broke in, winking, with an air of teasing comprehension. He, too, wore glasses.

"At your age," he said, handing her the candies, "I could see like a cat, I could thread needles at night, my grandmother always wanted me nearby … but now I'm old."

Eugenia nodded vaguely. "My friends … none of them have lenses," she said. Then, turning to the servant Rosaria, but speaking also for Don Vincenzo's benefit: "Just me … Nine diopters on one side and ten on the other … I am almost blind!" she said emphatically, sweetly.

"See how lucky you are," said Don Vincenzo, smiling, and to Rosaria: "How much salt?"

"Poor child!" the Amodios' maid commented as Eugenia left, happily. "It's the dampness that's ruined her. In that building it rains on us. Now Donna Rosa's bones ache. Give me a kilo of coarse salt and a packet of fine … "

"There you are."

"What a morning, eh, today, Don Vincenzo? It seems like summer already."

Walking more slowly than she had on the way there, Eugenia, without even realizing it, began to unwrap one of the two candies, and then put it in her mouth. It tasted of lemon. "I'll tell Aunt Nunzia that I lost it on the way," she proposed to herself. She was happy, it didn't matter to her if her aunt, good as she was, got angry. She felt someone take her hand, and recognized Luigino.

"You are really blind!" the boy said laughing. "And the glasses?"

"Mamma went to Via Roma to get them."

"I didn't go to school; it's a beautiful day, why don't we take a little walk?"

"You're crazy! Today I have to be good."

Luigino looked at her and laughed, with his mouth like a money box, stretching to his ears, contemptuous.

"What a rat's nest."

Instinctively Eugenia brought a hand to her hair.

"I can't see well, and Mamma doesn't have time," she answered meekly.

"What are the glasses like? With gold frames?" Luigino asked.

"All gold!" Eugenia answered, lying. "Bright and shiny!"

"Old women wear glasses," said Luigino.

"Also ladies, I saw them on Via Roma."

"Those are dark glasses, for sunbathing," Luigino insisted.

"You're just jealous. They cost eight thousand lire."

"When you have them, let me see them," said Luigino. "I want to see if the frame really is gold. You're such a liar," and he went off on his own business, whistling.

Reentering the courtyard, Eugenia wondered anxiously if her glasses would or wouldn't have a gold frame. In the negative case, what could she say to Luigino to convince him that they were a thing of value? But what a beautiful day! Maybe Mamma was about to return with the glasses wrapped in a package. Soon she would have them on her face. She would have ... A frenzy of blows fell on her head. A real fury. She seemed to collapse; in vain she defended herself with her hands. It was Aunt Nunzia, of course, furious because of her delay, and behind Aunt Nunzia was Pasqualino, like a madman, because he didn't believe her story about the candies. "Bloodsucker! You ugly little blind girl! And I who gave my life for this ingratitude ... You'll come to a bad end! Eight thousand lire no less. They bleed me dry, these scoundrels."

She let her hands fall, only to burst into a great lament. "Our Lady of Sorrows, holy Jesus, by the wounds in your ribs let me die!"

Eugenia wept, too, in torrents.

"Aunt, forgive me. Aunt ..."

"Uh ... uh ... uh ..." said Pasqualino, his mouth wide open.

"Poor child," said Donna Mariuccia, coming over to Eugenia, who didn't know where to hide her face, now streaked with red and tears at her aunt's rage. "She didn't do it on purpose, Nunzia, calm down," and to Eugenia: "Where've you got the candies?"

Eugenia answered softly, hopelessly, holding out one in her dirty hand: "I ate the other. I was hungry."

Before her aunt could move again, to attack the child, the

voice of the marchesa could be heard, from the fourth floor, where there was sun, calling softly, placidly, sweetly:

"Nunziata!"

Aunt Nunzia looked up, her face pained as that of the Madonna of the Seven Sorrows, which was at the head of her bed.

"Today is the first Friday of the month. Dedicate it to God."

"Marchesa, how good you are! These kids make me commit so many sins, I'm losing my mind, I …" And she collapsed her face between her paw-like hands, the hands of a worker, with brown, scaly skin.

"Is your brother not there?"

"Poor Aunt, she got you the eyeglasses, and that's how you thank her," said Mariuccia meanwhile to Eugenia, who was trembling.

"Yes, signora, here I am," answered Don Peppino, who until that moment had been half hidden behind the door of the basement room, waving a paper in front of the stove where the beans for lunch were cooking.

"Can you come up?"

"My wife went to get the eyeglasses for Eugenia. I'm watching the beans. Would you wait, if you don't mind."

"Then send up the child. I have a dress for Nunziata. I want to give it to her."

"May God reward you … very grateful," answered Don Peppino, with a sigh of consolation, because that was the only thing that could calm his sister. But looking at Nunziata, he realized that she wasn't at all cheered up. She continued to weep desperately, and that weeping had so stunned Pasqualino that the child had become quiet as if by magic, and was now licking the snot that dripped from his nose, with a small, sweet smile.

"Did you hear? Go up to the Signora Marchesa, she has a dress to give you," said Don Peppino to his daughter.

Eugenia was looking at something in the void, with her eyes that couldn't see: they were staring, fixed and large. She winced, and got up immediately, obedient.

"Say to her: 'May God reward you,' and stay outside the door."

"Yes, Papa."

"Believe me, Mariuccia," said Aunt Nunzia, when Eugenia had gone off, "I love that little creature, and afterward I'm sorry, as God is my witness, for scolding her. But I feel all the blood go to my head, believe me, when I have to fight with the kids. Youth is gone, as you see," and she touched her hollow cheeks. "Sometimes I feel like a madwoman."

"On the other hand, they have to vent, too," Donna Mariuccia answered. "They're innocent souls. They need time to weep. When I look at them, and think how they'll become just like us." She went to get a broom and swept a cabbage leaf out of the doorway. "I wonder what God is doing."

"It's new, brand-new! You hardly wore it!" said Eugenia, sticking her nose in the green dress lying on the sofa in the kitchen, while the marchesa went looking for an old newspaper to wrap it in.

The marchesa thought that the child really couldn't see, because otherwise she would have realized that the dress was very old and full of patches (it had belonged to her dead sister), but she refrained from commenting. Only after a moment, as she was coming in with the newspaper, she asked:

"And the eyeglasses your aunt got you? Are they new?"

"With gold frames. They cost eight thousand lire," Eugenia answered all in one breath, becoming emotional again at the thought of the honor she had received, "because I'm almost blind," she added simply.

"In my opinion," said the marchesa, carefully wrapping the dress in the newspaper, and then reopening the package because a sleeve was sticking out, "your aunt could have saved her money. I saw some very good eyeglasses in a shop near the Church of the Ascension, for only two thousand lire."

Eugenia blushed fiery red. She understood that the marchesa was displeased. "Each to his own position in life. We all must know our limitations," she had heard her say this many times, talking to Donna Rosa, when she brought her the washed clothes, and stayed to complain of her poverty.

"Maybe they weren't good enough. I have nine diopters," she replied timidly.

The marchesa arched an eyebrow, but luckily Eugenia didn't see it.

"They were good, I'm telling you," the Marchesa said obstinately, in a slightly harsher voice. Then she was sorry. "My dear," she said more gently, "I'm saying this because I know the troubles you have in your household. With that difference of six thousand lire, you could buy bread for ten days, you could buy … What's the use to you of seeing better? Given what's around you!" A silence. "To read, maybe, but do you read?"

"No, signora."

"But sometimes I've seen you with your nose in a book. A liar as well, my dear. That is no good."

Eugenia didn't answer again. She felt truly desperate, staring at the dress with her nearly white eyes.

"Is it silk?" she asked stupidly.

The marchesa looked at her, reflecting.

"You don't deserve it, but I want to give you a little gift," she said suddenly, and headed toward a white wooden wardrobe. At that moment the telephone, which was in the hall, began to ring, and instead of opening the wardrobe the marchesa went to answer it. Eugenia, oppressed by those words, hadn't even heard the old woman's consoling allusion, and as soon as she was alone she began to look around as far as her poor eyes allowed her. How many fine, beautiful things! Like the store on Via Roma! And there, right in front of her, an open balcony with a lot of small pots of flowers.

She went out onto the balcony. How much air, how much blue! The apartment buildings seemed to be covered by a blue veil, and below was the alley, like a ravine, with so many ants coming and going ... like her relatives. What were they doing? Where were they going? They went in and out of their holes, carrying big crumbs of bread, they were doing this now, had done it yesterday, would do it tomorrow, forever, forever. So many holes, so many ants. And around them, almost invisible in the great light, the world made by God, with the wind, the sun, and out there the purifying sea, so vast ... She was standing there, her chin planted on the iron railing, suddenly thoughtful, with an expression of sorrow, of bewilderment, that made her look ugly. She heard the sound of the marchesa's voice, calm, pious. In her hand, in her smooth ivory hand, the marchesa was holding a small book covered in black paper with gilt letters.

"It's the thoughts of the saints, my dear. The youth of today don't read anything, and so the world has changed course. Take it, I'm giving it to you. But you must promise to read a little every evening, now that you've got your glasses."

"Yes, signora," said Eugenia, in a hurry, blushing again

because the marchesa had found her on the balcony, and she took the book. Signora D'Avanzo regarded her with satisfaction.

"God wished to save you, my dear!" she said, going to get the package with the dress and placing it in her hands. "You're not pretty, anything but, and you already appear to be an old lady. God favors you, because looking like that you won't have opportunities for evil. He wants you to be holy, like your sisters!"

Although the words didn't really wound her, because she had long been unconsciously prepared for a life without joy, Eugenia was nevertheless disturbed by them. And it seemed to her, if only for a moment, that the sun no longer shone as before, and even the thought of the eyeglasses ceased to cheer her. She looked vaguely, with her nearly dead eyes, at a point on the sea, where the Posillipo peninsula extended like a faded green lizard. "Tell Papa," the marchesa continued, meanwhile, "that we won't do anything about the child's mattress today. My cousin telephoned, and I'll be in Posillipo all day."

"I was there once, too ..." Eugenia began, reviving at that name and looking, spellbound, in that direction.

"Yes? Is that so?" Signora D'Avanzo was indifferent, the name of that place meant nothing special to her. In her magisterial fashion, she accompanied the child, who was still looking toward that luminous point, to the door, closing it slowly behind her.

As Eugenia came down the last step and out into the courtyard, the shadow that had been darkening her forehead for a while disappeared, and her mouth opened in a joyful laugh, because she had seen her mother arriving. It wasn't hard to recognize that worn, familiar figure. She threw the dress on a chair and ran toward her.

"Mamma! The eyeglasses!"

"Gently, my dear, you'll knock me over!"

Immediately, a small crowd formed. Donna Mariuccia, Don Peppino, one of the Greborios, who had stopped to rest on a chair before starting up the stairs, the Amodios' maid, who was just then returning, and, of course, Pasqualino and Teresella, who wanted to see, too, and yelled, holding out their hands. Nunziata, for her part, was observing the dress that she had taken out of the newspaper, with a disappointed expression.

"Look, Mariuccia, it's an old rag ... all worn out under the arms!" she said, approaching the group. But who was paying attention to her? At that moment, Donna Rosa was extracting from a pocket in her dress the eyeglass case, and with infinite care opened it. On Donna Rosa's long red hand, a kind of very shiny insect with two giant eyes and two curving antennae glittered in a pale ray of sun amid those poor people, full of admiration.

"Eight thousand lire ... a thing like that!" said Donna Rosa, gazing at the eyeglasses religiously, and yet with a kind of rebuke.

Then, in silence, she placed them on Eugenia's face, as the child ecstatically held out her hands, and carefully arranged the two antennae behind her ears. "Now can you see?" Donna Rosa asked with great emotion.

Gripping the eyeglasses with her hands, as if in fear that they would be taken away from her, her eyes half closed and her mouth half open in a rapt smile, Eugenia took two steps backward, and stumbled on a chair.

"Good luck!" said the Amodios' maid.

"Good luck!" said the Greborio sister.

"She looks like a schoolteacher, doesn't she?" Don Peppino observed with satisfaction.

"Not even a thank you!" said Aunt Nunzia, looking bitterly at the dress. "With all that, good luck!"

"She's afraid, my little girl!" murmured Donna Rosa, heading toward the door of the basement room to put down her things. "She's put on the eyeglasses for the first time!" she said, looking up at the first-floor balcony, where the other Greborio sister was looking out.

"I see everything very tiny," said Eugenia, in a strange voice, as if she were speaking from under a chair. "Black, very black."

"Of course: the lenses are double. But do you see clearly?" asked Don Peppino. "That's the important thing. She's put on the glasses for the first time," he, too, said, addressing Cavaliere Amodio, who was passing by, holding an open newspaper.

"I'm warning you," the cavaliere said to Mariuccia, after staring at Eugenia for a moment, as if she were merely a cat, "that stairway hasn't been swept. I found some fish bones in front of the door!" And he went on, bent over, almost enfolded in his newspaper, reading an article about a proposal for a new pension law that interested him.

Eugenia, still holding on to the eyeglasses with her hands, went to the entrance to the courtyard to look outside into Vicolo della Cupa. Her legs were trembling, her head was spinning, and she no longer felt any joy. With her white lips she wished to smile, but that smile became a moronic grimace. Suddenly the balconies began to multiply, two thousand, a hundred thousand; the carts piled with vegetables were falling on her; the voices filling the air, the cries, the lashes, struck her head as if she were ill; she turned, swaying, toward the courtyard, and that terrible impression intensified. The courtyard was like a sticky funnel, with the narrow end toward the sky, its leprous walls crowded with derelict balconies; the arches of the basement dwellings black, with the lights bright in a circle around

Our Lady of Sorrows; the pavement white with soapy water; the cabbage leaves, the scraps of paper, the garbage and, in the middle of the courtyard, that group of ragged, deformed souls, faces pocked by poverty and resignation, who looked at her lovingly. They began to writhe, to become mixed up, to grow larger. They all came toward her, in the two bewitched circles of the eyeglasses. It was Mariuccia who first realized that the child was sick, and she tore off the glasses, because Eugenia, doubled over and moaning, was throwing up.

"They've gone to her stomach!" cried Mariuccia, holding her forehead. "Bring a coffee bean, Nunziata!"

"A grand total of a good eight thousand lire!" cried Aunt Nunzia, her eyes popping out of her head, running into the basement room to get a coffee bean from a can in the cupboard; and she held up the new eyeglasses, as if to ask God for an explanation. "And now they're wrong, too!"

"It's always like that, the first time," said the Amodios' maid to Donna Rosa calmly. "You mustn't be shocked; little by little one gets used to them."

"It's nothing, child, nothing, don't be scared!" But Donna Rosa felt her heart constrict at the thought of how unlucky they were.

Aunt Nunzia returned with the coffee bean, still crying: "A grand total of a good eight thousand lire!" while Eugenia, pale as death, tried in vain to throw up, because she had nothing left inside her. Her bulging eyes were almost crossed with suffering, and her old lady's face was bathed in tears, as if stupefied. She leaned on her mother and trembled.

"Mamma, where are we?"

"We're in the courtyard, my child," said Donna Rosa patiently; and the fine smile, between pity and wonder, that illuminated her eyes, suddenly lit up the faces of all those wretched people.

"She's half-blind!"

"She's a half-wit, she is!"

"Leave her alone, poor child, she's dazed," said Donna Mariuccia, and her face was grim with pity, as she went back into the basement apartment that seemed to her darker than usual.

Only Aunt Nunzia was wringing her hands:

"A grand total of a good eight thousand lire!"

FAMILY INTERIOR

～ ✑ ✑ ～

Anastasia Finizio, the older daughter of Angelina Finizio and the late Ernesto, one of Chiaia's leading hairdressers, who only a few years earlier had retired to a sunny and tranquil enclosure in the cemetery of Poggioreale, had just returned from High Mass (it was Christmas Day) at Santa Maria degli Angeli, in Monte di Dio, and still hadn't made up her mind to take off her hat. Tall and thin, like all the Finizios, with the same meticulous, glittering elegance, which contrasted sharply with the dullness and indefinable decrepitude of their horsey figures, Anastasia paced up and down the bedroom she shared with her sister, Anna, unable to contain a visible agitation. Only a few minutes earlier, everything had been indifference and peace, coldness and resignation in her heart of a woman on the verge of forty, who, almost without realizing it, had lost every hope of personal happiness and adapted fairly easily to a man's life—all responsibility, accounts, work. In the same place where her father had styled the most demanding heads of Naples, she had a knitwear shop, and with that she supported the household: mother, aunt, sister, two brothers, one of whom was about to get married. Apart from the pleasure of dressing like a sophisticated woman of the big city, she didn't know or wish for anything else.

And now in an instant, she was no longer herself. Not that she was ill, not at all, but she felt a happiness that wasn't really happiness so much as a revival of the imagination she had believed dead, a disorientation. The fact that she had reached an excellent position in life, that she dressed well, and the many moral satisfactions she gained from maintaining all those people—these had disappeared, or almost, like a whirlwind, confronted by the hope of being young and a woman again. In her brain, at that moment, there was true confusion, as if an entire crowd were shouting and lamenting, pleading for mercy, before someone who had come to announce, in an equivocal way, something extraordinary. She was still stunned by the bellowing of the organ, by the furor of the hymns, dazzled by the sparkle of gold and silver on the reds and whites of the sacred vestments, by the twinkling lights; her head was still heavy with the penetrating scent of lilies and roses, mixed with the funereal odor of incense, when, upon reaching the entrance, and stretching out her arms toward the plain, everyday air, she had run into Lina Stassano, the sister of her future sister-in-law, and thus learned that, after years of absence, a certain Antonio Laurano, a youth she had once considered, was back in Naples. "His health isn't bad, but he says he's tired of being at sea, and wants to find a job in Naples. He said to me: If you see Anastasia Finizio give her a special greeting." That was all; it could be much, or nothing, but this time—as if something had broken in her rigid mental mechanism, the old control, all the defenses of a race forced to greater and greater sacrifices because there would be hell to pay if they weren't made—Anastasia, who had always been so cold and cautious, let herself go, as if bewitched, into the digressions of a feeling as obscure as it was extraordinary.

"Ah, Madonna!" she was saying in her mind, without being

aware herself of this mysterious conversation she was having. "If it were true! If Lina Stassano isn't wrong ... if that really is Antonio's feeling for me! But why couldn't it be? What's odd about it? I'm not bad-looking ... and I can't even say I'm old, although twenty years have gone by. I have no illusions; I look at reality, I do look. I'm independent ... I have a position ... money ... He's tired of sailing ... maybe disappointed ... he wants to settle in Naples ... I could help him ... Perhaps he needs security, affection ... he's not looking for a girl but a woman. And I, on the other hand, what sort of life do I lead? House and shop, shop and house. I'm not like my sister, Anna, who still wears her hair down and plays the piano. The young men, now, no longer notice me, and if I didn't dress well and use an expensive perfume, they wouldn't even bother to say hello. I'm not old yet, but I'm about to get old. I didn't realize it, but it's so. Either Antonio really does have feelings for me, loves me, and needs me, or I'm lost. I'll always have my clothes, of course, but even the statues in church have clothes, and the people in photographs have clothes."

She'd never spoken this way before; her language tended toward comments about income and outflow, or, at most, interesting observations about this year's fashions. Therefore she was astonished and discouraged, like someone who for the first time sees a wretched and silent town, and is told that she has been living there, thinking that she has been seeing palaces and gardens where there was only gravel and nettles; and Anastasia, considering in a flash that her life had been nothing but servitude and sleep, and was now about to decline, stopped walking and looked around her with an air of bewilderment.

The window of the room, which was large and clean, but sparsely furnished, with two iron bedsteads, a wardrobe, and some chairs set here and there on the redbrick floor, and above the beds and the wardrobe an olive branch from the previous Easter—that window was open, and from outside a deep blue light entered, intense and at the same time cold, as if the sky from which it came were completely new to this earth, without the old intimate warmth of long ago. Not a cloud could be seen, not the smallest spot, or even the sun, and that fragment of walls and cornices that appeared at the level of the windowsill—faded, ethereal, like a drawing—seemed the world's dribbles rather than its reality. Not a voice or a cry could be heard from the inhabitants of Naples, and in that moment Anastasia, standing near the window, her brow slightly furrowed, her heart heavy—whether with hope or anguish she no longer knew—looked down, almost not recognizing the places or the people. It seemed to her that the upward-sloping street, three stories below her, had a mysterious depth and sadness. The pavement, still dark from the night's rain, was strewn with all the wood shavings and refuse from Christmas Eve. Many people were going to Mass or returning, and, meeting, stopped for a moment to exchange good wishes, a greeting, but one had to pay attention to distinguish the voices ("Merry Christmas!" "Good wishes to you and all your family!" "Same to you!"). Thanks to the beauty of the day, windows were open as far as the eye could see, and here and there one could glimpse a narrow black iron headboard, the white coverlet of a bed, the gilded oval frame of a dark painting, a chandelier's glittering branch, the amber procession of gilded mullions in a living room. There was plenty of activity going on in the kitchens, but the men were all free, some shaving, some collapsed, inert, against a windowsill, some staring out across the red flowerpots on a balcony. One, cigarette in hand, his face pockmarked by the passions and boredom of Neapolitan youth, gazed with indifference or melancholy at the exaggerated depth of the sky. Listening carefully, one could hear snatches of song—*"cchiù bello 'e te"* or *"'o sole mio,"* "more beautiful than you," "my own sun"—but a silence persisted in the houses, as in the streets, that was not cheerful, as if the Christian celebration spreading temporarily over the anthill of streets were not so much a celebration as the flag of an unknown army raised at the center of a burned and devastated village. Dressed in his best, a boy of about thirteen, hands in his pockets, looked out from a balcony next to the Finizios' window, with the grave, yellowish face of the seriously ill, spitting while he daydreamed. From time to time, a dog passed by in a hurry.

"That life would have been a dream," Anastasia continued to think, trying to harden herself, to overcome that vague fear, that weakness and confusion of her thoughts, pierced by such an unusual and cruel light, "like a lane that seems to be trailing off out in a dirt field, and instead, unexpectedly, opens into a square full of people, with music playing. Suddenly, you see, I would go and live in a house of my own. I wouldn't go to the shop anymore. Yes, I never liked that life. I felt that someday it would have to end. Certainly I would get a satisfactory price for the shop. I can ask two million, even more, for that hole-in-the-wall in Chiaia. With two million, I could afford a place near here, so every day I'd come see Mamma. Three rooms and a terrace, with a view of San Martino." She saw herself busy in those rooms, on a summer morning, hanging out clothes, and singing. But although she remained glued to this image, she did not extract any joy from it. It was as if she were witnessing someone else's happiness. She thought also of summer evenings, when they would eat on the terrace, in the glow of an electric light hidden in the pergola; it would illuminate her hardened worker's hands on the table, and make Antonio's beautiful teeth sparkle in the darkness. And now thinking of those teeth, she saw, amazed, that all her intoxication originated there, in that mouth, younger than her own, indeed, young, with that health and youth that she had never possessed. And how had so many years passed— twenty, thirty—without her knowing this, without her wanting or even suspecting it? And why—now—did she desire it?

She calculated rapidly how old he was, thirty-two, and, comparing it to her own age, said aloud: "Impossible."

She was still looking down, but her face was different: her brow wrinkled in the effort to get control of herself, her pink eyelids lowering, with the mechanical movement of a doll, over eyes distressed by humiliation. In the face of that certainty, everything that was disagreeable about her came to the surface, like the foam on the sea. Impossible, impossible! And her lips tightened, her cheeks, of an orange-pink color, caved in, making her forehead appear larger and bleaker, and the arch of her eyebrows more pretentious. Terribly unhappy, the Finizios' older daughter had no expression, and her saddest moments were also the most perfectly banal. There was some obtuseness in her mind, that was all, a torpor, although sometimes she was aware of it, like the effect of an effort sustained over many centuries. She couldn't think, live. Something was alive in her, and yet she couldn't express it. This was her goodness, her strength, this incapacity to understand and want a life of her own. Only in remembering could she, from time to time, see, and then immediately that light, that landscape was extinguished. She remembered Antonio as if it were yesterday: not tall, but solid as a column, with brown hair and dark skin, and those sad eyes, of a man, and the mouth with the crowded teeth, white when he smiled; and the affectionate ways, as if marked by compassion, that he had with everyone, as if he were always returning from far away: "How are you, Anastasia?" "What do you want, life is the same ... " "True, but it could be better." (And who knows what he was alluding to with that "better.") "Come and see us sometime, it would be a pleasure." That was all she knew to say to him, when they met, and with an idiotic, haughty expression. As if she were happy, as if her work were enough for her, and the satisfaction of supporting the whole family since her father died, and all those clothes that she made could console her. Instead, it wasn't true. Countless times she would willingly have thrown away all those satisfactions, and gone to be a servant in his house, and serve him, serve him forever, the way a true woman serves a man.

Bells tolled in two or three churches at once, and, at that terrible and familiar sound, which spoke of heaven and not of life, Anastasia roused herself. Her eyes filled with tears, and leaving the window she resumed walking up and down the room, her attention rapt, while she repeated mechanically: "The way a true woman serves a man ... Yes, nothing else."

"Anastasia! Anastasia!"

"Where is Anastasia?"

It was Anna and Petrillo. Her only sister, pale-faced at the age of eighteen, with the beauty of ordinary roses, her large, gentle, protruding eyes at that moment filled by a lively smile, and Petrillo, with his air of a studious cockroach, eyeglasses planted in the middle of his small green face, rushed into the room where Anastasia Finizio was pacing restlessly, absorbed in those new thoughts. In fact, the one who rushed in was Anna, in a white dress that spread around her narrow hips as she ran, one hand, almost out of habit, at her blond hair, tied by a blue ribbon.

Petrillo, in a man's suit even though he was only sixteen, was a few steps behind, holding on to his eyeglasses, because one lens was broken and the least movement might cause it to fall out.

"Did you see who's arrived?"

"No," answered Anastasia, returning to the window and pretending to look out. She took off her gloves and put them back on, with her heart jumping out of her chest, and all of her aging blood rushing to her face, imagining she would hear, in a moment, that name. Never had she been so embarrassed. But she was wrong.

"Don Liberato, Donn'Amelia's brother, from Salerno. He sent someone to say that he's coming to see us after lunch."

"Yes?" said Anastasia, relieved to feel that her heart was beating more regularly, her head cooling. At the same time it was as if that shadow, that sadness which in all its extraordinary imaginings had continually emerged to obscure the colors, had solidified, and she sat down, like a beggar, on the chair in the corner of the room. Her agitation vanished suddenly, and she was able to look at her siblings.

"Why? Donn'Amelia isn't coming?" she asked calmly.

"She was sick all night," Anna answered, going to look at herself in the windowpane, with an indolence that was due not merely to southern frivolity but also to the languor of lifeless blood, "and the doctor came this morning, too. Didn't you hear?"

"Anastasia doesn't hear anything except money," said Petrillo maliciously, and he waited for an irritated response, but his sister said nothing.

"Mamma asks," Anna continued idly, "if you would take the green glasses with the gold trim out of the chest. Dora Stassano and Giovannino are coming for lunch."

This Giovannino was Anna's fiancé, a bookstore clerk, a short man with a red mustache, and although Anastasia didn't think much of him, her heart constricted as she thought how her sister, twenty years younger, could speak easily about things that instead caused her confusion and torment. Even the thought of having to bend over the chest in her mother's room, in her good clothes, to take out of its dusty interior the glasses so dear to Signora Finizio that she used them only on special occasions increased that inner chill. All Anna did was play the piano and take walks, for Anna duties … annoying things … didn't exist. A nice life, Anna's.

"Petrillo, go out a moment," she said in a flat voice.

"I've just done my nails," Anna said timidly. "I'm sorry."

Anastasia didn't respond this time, either. While the boy left, whistling, with the superior attitude he'd acquired some months earlier, ever since he'd started to exchange a few serious words with a girl, Anastasia took off her blue wool coat, which had seen all that great joy, and then those bewilderments, that suffering, and laid it on the bed. With the same care, she took the blue hat off her head, removing the pins first. She opened her purse, also blue, took out a very white, scented handkerchief, and held it for a moment under her nose. Finally she sat down on the bed and, without using her hands, took off her shoes, which she pushed aside. In doing all these things, she was wasting time; there was a kind of silence in her, and also an obscure apprehension. That moment of emotion minutes earlier had disappeared completely, vanished, and she felt her younger sister looking at her, in fact observing her, with the large, beautiful, slightly surprised eyes of youths destined to die prematurely (Anna had a weak lung), and she had a very faint sensation of shame, of guilt, as if she were already old, and all those fabrics, powders, and scents that she put on her person constituted a theft, a sin, something that was taken away from the natural need of her brothers, of Anna. A thousand years seemed to pass before her sister left the room, before she stopped looking at her.

"Mamma asks if you will also go to the kitchen for a moment and give them a hand. I have to look over the songs."

"Yes, I'm coming," Anastasia answered calmly. "I'm just going to rest a moment, then I'll come."

But her sister wasn't paying attention to her anymore. Near the open window, she was looking at her reflection in the glass, through which other balconies could be seen, and turning her pretty blond head slightly, she adjusted the blue ribbon and sang softly, *Tutto è passato!* It's all over! in her dull, gentle voice.

To get to the kitchen, Anastasia had to go out into a wide, bare hallway, onto which all four rooms of the house opened, and illuminated at the far end by a window looking onto a garden. Now that window was wide open, and the crudely whitewashed frame enclosed a dark blue sky so smooth and shining that it seemed fake. That morning an enormous beauty was in the air, and by comparison the houses and lives of men appeared strangely poor, shabby. And so Aunt Nana, who was hunched over, washing the floor, seemed to Anastasia's disturbed gaze a real monstrosity. This woman, her mother's older sister, after an idle youth, full of frivolous endeavors, and in continual expectation of a husband, had gradually had to resign herself, as happened among the women of the petty bourgeoisie, to a servile and silent life in the house of the married sister. Bring up this child, bring up this other one—there had no longer been time for personal occupations and thoughts. Over the years she had become almost completely deaf, so that she no longer grasped the scoldings or the laughter that from time to time came at her expense. Her obsession was newspapers, which she read avidly at night, lingering in particular on stories of passion, on the more prominent love stories: suicides and homicides for love, injuries, rapes, when there were not, as she preferred, notices of famous people's engagements, weddings of princes and rulers, and, in short, the luxury and beauty of the world, mixed in with the happiness of the flesh. Then everything in her puffy, false, putrid-yellow face lit up, making her terrible eyes even blacker and shinier: the eyes of a woman who hasn't been able to live, but still could, and there alone she could be heard chuckling: "Youth, ah, youth, what joy!" She had always been short in stature, but now she seemed more than short, shrunken and twisted, like ancient trees at the heart of some forest. She always wore black, and on Sundays and holidays she dabbed her cheeks with rouge. Seeing her, Anastasia felt that sadness, too confused to be defined, increase, that disgust and at the same time pity for herself and the life she lived, that mute longing for a sweeter day which had been whispering in her ear, and she said:

"Precisely this morning you have to be so dutiful, Aunt Nana? Don't you feel how cold it is?"

"Beautiful, beautiful," answered Nana, getting up humbly and all excited, her eyes on the window. She had understood "beautiful." "Very beautiful day," she said, "made just for the young." And again she lowered her gaze to the floor. Once, she would have envied Anastasia her height and her nice clothes, because as a young woman she had been peevish and mean. But life, confining her to the lowest positions, had triumphed over those flaws, and now there was no one humbler than Nana, and inclined to be satisfied by the happiness of others. For Anastasia, then, she felt true adoration. Ultimately, it was Anastasia, with her work, who maintained her, and who knows where she would have ended up, poor Nana, if God had not blessed Anastasia's work.

In his room, bleak and cold as his sister's, and, like it, cursorily furnished, Eduardo, the older brother, was shaving in front of a small mirror attached to the window. As tall as Anastasia, and terribly thin, he had a chest hollowed like the moon, resembling all those of his ilk. But now he was cured, although secretly he still coughed something up, and in fact he, too, was about to marry, not to mention that he had been promised a temporary position at City Hall. Having seen his sister passing in the mirror, he called out in a shrill, pleading voice:

"Anastasia, my shirts!"

"They're already ironed!" Anastasia answered. "Next to the socks."

And she was about to go on, when she noticed, as if seeing it for the first time, his long back, his flattened, feeble figure, and she thought of a half-desiccated spider that sometimes hung from a web and appeared to move in the wind, and then one realized it was only a shadow. Similarly, Eduardo lived the life of a man only in appearance. Here if you saw him shave and ask shrilly for his shirts, he was a man ... As her gaze fell on the two beds, Eduardo's and Petrillo's, she recalled that in two months they would be replaced by a single big bed. The expenses for the furniture were Dora Stassano's; she worked as a dressmaker and earned pretty well, but Anastasia, too, would contribute, and she and Dora Stassano would have to support the children who would come, with long backs and the faces of miniature old horses. Anna, on the other hand, was not making such a good marriage, because Giovannino Bocca, the clerk, would never earn much, but her mother, because of Anna's delicate health, and fearing that death would take her away before she could enjoy herself, was determined to make her happy: and Anastasia alone, with the help of that clerk, would have to support the little children, with faces white as a winter rose and slightly protruding, astonished eyes. But she didn't linger on that detail: as a workhorse has the sensation that his burden is increasing from minute to minute, and his legs are folding under him, but his gentle eyes can't look back, so she couldn't see from which direction this enormous and useless life flowed over her, and knew only that she had to bear it. She thought for a moment how different the rooms of the house would be in spring: here Eduardo with Dora; in the sisters' room Anna with her husband. She, Anastasia, would go and sleep with her mother, while Petrillo would be settled on a cot in the dining room. In the past, when her father was alive, no one would have foreseen these changes, no one would have thought that Eduardo and Anna, marrying, would stay in the house. She recalled suddenly how she liked her room, when she was younger, and the endless chatter with Anna, between the beds, on summer nights, with the moonlight on their feet, the low laughter when the name of this or that man was mentioned. Unnoticed, that whispering had ceased.

As she passed the black box of the intercom, it rang. "Hello," said Anastasia.

"Your brother's fiancée is here," the porter's voice informed her from below.

In that home (because they still didn't know what type Petrillo's girl was) the official fiancée was Dora Stassano. So Anastasia said right away:

"Dora Stassano, happy Christmas to you and all your family."

"Who is it? Doruccia? Tell her to come up," cried Eduardo with the shaving brush in hand, turning his feverish eyes toward her.

"Eduardo says come up if you want," Anastasia reported. And after a moment: "Yes, he's expecting you. We're all here. Anna and Petrillo, too." She hung up the intercom receiver. "She's coming," she said, turning toward Eduardo's room.

In the kitchen, all four burners of the stove had been lighted. There wasn't enough coal (the gas was used only for coffee), and Signora Finizio had needed to add some wood, which had filled the space with an acrid smoke. A ray of sun, entering through the open window, lightly rippled that massive gray veil upon which millions of colored spots sparkled. Her eyes red, half closed because they stung, Signora Finizio, a lively woman, all bone, with red hair and a shrewd, loving face, moved with incredible agility, given her fifty-eight years, from one burner to the next. Seeing Anastasia, she cried:

"Please, dear daughter, have a quick look at the broth, while I finish the kneading."

It seemed to Signora Finizio, sometimes, that Anastasia wasted time in futile things, but she didn't dare to protest openly, for it appeared to her that the sort of sleep in which her daughter was sunk, and which allowed them all to live and expand peacefully, might at any moment, for a trifle, break. She had no liking for Anastasia (her beloved was Anna), but she valued her energy and, with it, her docility, that practical spirit joined to such resigned coldness. She was always amazed that her daughter was so resigned, but of course it was part of God's plan.

Anastasia went to get an apron hanging behind a door, among the brooms, and she tied it in front. But instead of going to the stove she washed her hands at the sink, and said:

"You look at the broth, Mamma, I'll take care of the kneading."

"Thank you, dear daughter," the mother said, with a rapid smile; and for a moment stood looking at her, as her large hands plunged into the pond of water and flour, feeling that obscure sense of pity and celebration, of remorse and joy, that always gripped her upon observing Anastasia's perfect, unchangeable ugliness, her rigid, expressionless features, like those of a fork. She was silently comparing that ugliness with the memory she had of herself as a girl, with the image of Anna, so luminous in her weakness, and smiled without knowing it.

"Your sister doesn't want to do anything," she said aloud.

"Anna's young, Mamma," Anastasia answered without looking up, as if she felt that gaze. "And she's never been too healthy."

"That's also true," said Signora Finizio, full of emotion. And she added impulsively and with a tinge of melancholy, "So often I say to myself: What will become of that daughter of mine the day Anastasia wants to marry? Will the eyes of her husband be enough to protect her? Because, some time or other, that day may come."

"You're joking, Mamma," Anastasia said in a slightly altered voice. "I'm not pretty."

Signora Finizio smiled again, and as Anastasia, looking at her, had misinterpreted that smile, she didn't want to disappoint her, and changed the subject.

"Don Liberato sent the servant to tell me he is coming to see us after lunch. He's arrived from Salerno. Bless us, I think Donn'Amelia is very ill."

"May the Lord have mercy on her," Anastasia confined herself to saying.

Signora Finizio was never at rest. Like her arms, her thoughts were never still, and she needed to shift, always biting into this subject or that. So, after glancing at the broth, she turned and said:

"I also heard from the Lauranos that their son came back last night from Genoa. I didn't want to tell you because I thought you'd feel bad. It seems that he's also engaged."

And she quietly observed her daughter's long face, which had become horribly hard and unpleasant in her efforts to control herself. Signora Finizio's lips lengthened into a very thin smile. Her youth had quickly run its course, and she didn't easily forgive anyone who wished to avoid the law that she had been subjected to. She was constantly irritated by Anastasia's secret intentions, her lack of humility, by seeing her live so independently, almost a lady, while she herself led a servile life.

"It's better this way, don't you think?" she insisted.

Anastasia didn't answer; she went to the sideboard to get some flour, and for a few moments, although she wished to, Signora Finizio couldn't see her daughter's face. But she already knew she had hurt her enough.

"May I? Ooh, what smoke! Merry Christmas to all!"

Dora Stassano, in the kitchen doorway, showed her face, common, thin, and eager, the olive skin made greener by the red of her scarf. "Can I give you a hand?"

"Shoo … shoo …" Signora Finizio cried playfully. She somewhat regretted what she had said to Anastasia, but she remained cheerful. "Everybody out. When my daughter and I work we don't want anyone in the way."

Dora Stassano was a small woman in a bright-green coat trimmed with golden fur, wearing green gloves and shoes, and

Anna's charming blond head, along with Eduardo's ugly smiling face, could just be glimpsed behind her.

"Mamma, will you let us see the dessert?" asked Eduardo.

"You, hurry up, if you don't want to miss the last Mass," his mother cried to him. "This family of mine is filling up with heretics," she said, turning to Dora. "Except Anastasia, who never fails in her Christian duties, and every morning peeks into church before she opens the shop. I want to know who honors God in this house. Look at him, at the age of thirty, he has to be led by the neck to the last Mass. And his siblings follow his example. At least you, Dora Stassano, have done your duty?"

"Last night we were all at Santa Maria degli Angeli, if that's what you mean," the girl answered.

"Good, good!" Like Nana, Signora Finizio was becoming a little deaf, and so she said even the most delicate things in a loud voice.

"The church was so crowded it was suffocating," Dora continued, in the contrite and mischievous tone of one who says things that, in essence, she doesn't care about but likes others to believe. "I didn't see you, Mamma, you must have been farther up front. But I saw the Torri sisters, then Donn'Amelia with her brother, and the servant behind, and when the Elevation came Donn'Amelia began weeping. More toward the front were the Lauranos, all of them, including the son."

There was a brief silence at that word "son."

The thought that Donn'Amelia, a good neighbor, was in her last days (she had a serious heart ailment) moved and at the same time cheered Signora Finizio, who in her meager existence drew obscure consolation from the misfortunes of others, and in fact was undecided for a moment whether to stay with that subject or the second. But the second was more important. She still didn't feel at ease concerning Anastasia's feelings.

"So, Antonio really is back?" she cried. "I'm pleased. And he's getting married?"

This question, who knows why, no one answered. The smoke in the kitchen, pierced by a thin ray of sun, glittered like gold. There was a sensation of happiness and of expectation in all of them, even, impossible as it might seem, in the unhappy Anastasia. And now advancing through that ray of sun, almost crawling on the floor, was the horrible body and the waxy smiling face of Nana. With comical gestures, leaning on her man's walking stick, she indicated that someone had come; like a dog, humble and content, she pulled on the motionless Anna's dress.

She finally understood.

"Oh, Giovannino!" she said, turning her head, suddenly animated and blissful. And she disappeared into the hall.

"They love each other, ah. They're in love. They're so in love. Fine thing, fine thing youth is," and, looking this way and that, Nana spoke by herself, as always, partly because no one paid attention to her, while Eduardo had sneaked away, in secret from his mother, to open the sideboard and see the dessert.

Taking advantage of that moment, Dora Stassano went up to Anastasia and, looking at her with eyes burning like black fire and encircled by just a thread of melancholy, said in an undertone:

"Greetings from Laurano."

Again the bells began to ring, but this time only in her mind. Anastasia cleaned her flour-covered hands on a rag and, head lowered, said coldly:

"Same to him."

"I know that you once entertained a thought," Dora said, staring at her.

"We were all young," Anastasia answered.

"He also told me that, one of these days, if he had time, he would stop by for a moment."

"He can come when he wants, it will always be a pleasure for us."

Signora Finizio, with her long pointed nose over the boiling pot, felt that around the table, in the smoke and cold of that holiday morning, there was a mood different from the normal one; she realized that Anastasia Finizio, even if her appearance was, as usual, indifferent and serious, was disturbed. With true anguish, she understood that the equilibrium, the peace of the family would be in danger if the pillar of that house softened. She would have liked to get rid of Dora Stassano, but she didn't want to fight with Eduardo, and then Dora was important. Nor was it good to annoy Anastasia. Humiliate her, she had to, that was all, humiliate her and, indirectly, delicately, recall her to her duties. In thinking this, she had to make an effort to repress a torrent of anger, and a hidden suffering (to this she was reduced, begging from her children), which suffocated her. Smiling, she turned to Dora:

"And Antonio, how was he? He's not coming to see us? At one time he did come."

"Yes, he told me that he'll come one day soon," Dora shouted in one ear.

"Ah, good, good!" said Signora Finizio, with an expression almost of lament. And, as she turned her gaze, seeing that Eduardo had taken the dessert down from the sideboard, and was furtively running a finger over it, then licking it, she shouted with savage irritation: "Get out, you shameless boy, get out!"

Eduardo obeyed, happy, partly because he knew that her shout wasn't directed at him, and he left the kitchen, pulling Dora Stassano along with him.

"I feel exasperated today, who knows why," Signora Finizio complained when she was left alone with Anastasia.

"You must be tired, Mamma."

"Maybe. These holidays are a terrible strain, only the young enjoy them. As for us, at our age, there's nothing that can bring us comfort. To serve, serve until death, that's what's left for us. Everything we do is for others."

In the dining room, the table was set with all the best silverware, plates, and glasses. There were eight places because Dora Stassano's only sister had also been invited, and with her Giovannino Bocca, Anna's fiancé. On the sideboard, among some bunches of pink flowers, the famous green glasses were lined up, twelve in all, and, farther back, the porcelain plate with the Sicilian cassata could be glimpsed. The fruit was arranged on a lower table.

But the most interesting thing was the crèche, an enormous construction of cardboard and cork. It was Eduardo's doing. Every year, with the eagerness of a child, he started work on it two months before the holiday, shrieking like a madman if someone disturbed him. This year, since things were going well for the family, it was bigger than ever before, taking up the whole corner between the balcony and the kitchen door, where usually there was a small console table with a scene of Venice above it. Because of this construction, the room seemed smaller and more cheerful. It really was a work carried out with painstaking and patient love, in which all a man's capacities and intelligence were on display. The background had been made from an immense sheet of royal-blue cardboard sprinkled with perhaps two hundred stars cut out of silver and gold paper, and attached with glue. The grotto, dug into the arc of an undulating, peaceful hill that somewhat resembled Naples, wasn't large, and you had to stoop down to make out the figures inside, which were barely thumb-size. St. Joseph and the Virgin, both molded with the rock they were sitting on, had bright pink faces and hands, and, bending over the manger, seemed to be grimacing horribly, like people who are dying. The child, much bigger than his parents (in part for symbolic reasons), was instead smooth and pale, and slept with one leg over the other, like a man. His face showed nothing, other than an apathetic smile, as if he were saying, "This is the world," or something like that. A tiny electric light illuminated the stable, where everything, from the child's flesh to the animals' noses, expressed passivity and a harsh languor.

Outside the grotto it was much more beautiful. The shepherds were a real army, motionlessly inundating that small mountain. They appeared to be going up and down the slopes, looking out of one of the white houses built into the rock (in the style of southern towns), or leaning over a well, or sitting at the table of a country inn; or, finally, to be sleeping, waking, walking, courting a girl, or selling (and you could see their mouths opened in a cry) a basket of fish, or resoling shoes (sitting at a cobbler's bench), or performing a tarantella, while another, crouching in a corner with a mischievous air, touched a guitar. Many, standing near a donkey or some sheep, had their arms raised to indicate a distant point in that blue paper, or shielded their eyes with one hand to protect them from the bright light of an angel, who had dropped from a tree, with a strip of paper on which was written "Hosanna!" or "Peace on earth to men of good will!" Finally, there were two elegant cafés, on the model of those in Piazza dei Martiri, with small nickel-plated tables on the sidewalk, and red-wheeled carriages that drove up and down, carrying ladies holding fans and white parasols.

Every so often someone stopped piously in front of that simulacrum of the Divinity, and observed this or that animal, or even picked one up—a sheep or a rooster—and examined it from all sides with curiosity.

The room was already full of family members, chatting as they waited for lunch, and the younger, like Petrillo and Anna, jokingly played some notes on the piano.

"Murolo is always Murolo," Eduardo was saying, while Anna, standing in front of the piano, played now this key, now that one, enunciating, with her mouth closed, the words of *Core 'ngrato*— Ungrateful Heart—the same that could be heard in the morning, rising here and there in the narrow streets from phonographs and radios:

Tutto è passato!

"That's enough, enough of these sad things," said Dora. "Today is supposed to be joyful. This is the year that everyone's getting married," she added, winking at Anastasia.

Anastasia, standing near the balcony, elegantly dressed, but with a long, melancholy expression, because she was still thinking of this life and of Antonio, gave her a glance full of gratitude and at the same time of anxiety, feeling herself revive yet again in those words. Therefore, she, too, was considered young; for her, too, there was hope! And that obstruction in her heart, that confused shame, that opposition to thinking things not suitable for her—maybe those were the mistake, and not the hope of living.

Aunt Nana's walking stick could be heard pounding everywhere. The poor woman, like a frog that happens into a circle

of butterflies and no longer cares about the boredom of its existence, was eager to seize on some voice, a single note in that
jumbled, gentle chatter, which would restore to her a connec-
tion with what she had long ago lost. Youth and love tormented
her with curiosity, and she examined faces, unable to hear the
voices, and muttered and laughed continuously, approving what
she thought she grasped.

"Oh, oh, what joy, what beauty is youth!" On her yellow
cheeks, in honor of youth, she had put a little rouge, and now
her terrible eyes were burning. "Oh, oh, what joy!"

"As for me," Giovannino Bocca, a young man with a car-
rot-colored mustache and big red ears, was saying, "as for me,
I think the Naples team is on its way to becoming good. But it
needs money ... yeah ... a lot of money."

"Also, our stadium needs to be renovated ..." Eduardo
observed, in a bored tone, and, approaching the piano, he
moved some scores around on the music stand. "It seems that
Casa Ricordi is having a revival. Have you heard what great
songs they have this year?"

"Here's one that's pretty good for dancing," said Anna. "Listen ..."

"It really makes you want to dance," and Dora Stassano
spun around vivaciously, while Petrillo observed her.

There was nothing extraordinary here. Anastasia knew and
pitied the young, who were sickly and unemployed, with few
ambitions, few dreams, a scant life; and yet, at that moment,
they appeared to her beautiful, healthy, happy, rich in dreams
and possibilities that would one day be fulfilled; and she shared
in that joy, even though she knew that it didn't belong to her,
that she was remote from it. Her brain knew this, but her blood
no longer knew it. Now at any moment, the young man would

arrive; the door would open and he would come right in, and, sitting at the table, without looking at her, would ask, a little self-conscious, a little emotional: "Well, how are we doing? And you, Anastasia, still at the shop? I heard you're getting married, too, is it true?" Oh, my God! Everything would change, after that conversation, the afternoon would be different from the usual, and the evening as well; maybe, talking to Anna in their room, late at night, she would tell her everything. And the next day would be another day, and the day after, too. The news would spread. "Anastasia's getting married … It seems she's marrying the Lauranos' older son … He's younger than she is, but men have these odd passions … He'll never leave her … He's jealous." No, jealous was too much, even if it warmed her heart. They would say, instead: "She's almost old, but he loves her just the same … It was a feeling he'd had for years … He admired her."

"To the table, to the table!" Signora Finizio cried just then, entering the room with a tray that held the steaming white porcelain soup tureen, full of the countless little yellow eyes of the broth.

With a great scraping of chairs, the table was soon occupied. Prayers were recited, good wishes repeated, and Anastasia felt a happiness so intoxicating and strange that, suddenly, without saying a word, she went around kissing everyone, mother, siblings, in-laws, and when she returned to her place, her eyes shining with tears, she couldn't breathe.

They had finished the appetizer, and were tasting the first tagliolini, with small sighs of satisfaction (only Anastasia, completely absorbed in her dream, had barely touched her spoon), when the contentedness and peace of that hour were pierced by an indescribable noise, a broad and secret wave of sounds, of sighs rising from the courtyard overlooked by the dining room balcony, and from the building's stairways and open loggia. Petrillo, who had jumped up to go and see, held his breath for a moment, then erupted in an excited "*Madonna!*" at which they all or almost all rose abruptly to go to the windows, while Nana, who, her mouth full, and intent on chewing, hadn't noticed anything, continued to repeat, "Oh, what joy, oh, what joy!"

In front of one of the two doors on the third floor, where Donn'Amelia lived, there was a small crowd from which rose weeping and laments. That weeping came from the servant and one or two neighbors, while the others confined themselves to remarking on the fate that had cut off the life of Donn'Amelia, still young.

In a rush, Eduardo opened the balcony door, and they all went out, despite the cold air, to see better. Indeed, all the tenants had done the same.

The balconies overlooking the courtyard were crowded with people who had interrupted Christmas lunch to observe with surprise and a certain disquiet how death had passed over that house, and on a holiday, too. Silence had fallen on the Finizio family, which was then broken by remarks such as:

"Who would have thought!"

"Poor Donn'Amelia!"

"Still, she was ill."

"Don Liberato was in time to see her."

From one person in the crowd came this message, directed toward a distant balcony: "She died with the blessing of the Holy Father!"

"Lucky her!" responded another voice. "Now her suffering is over."

"This life is a torment," another lamented.

"Punishment."

"Hear the bells!" (And in fact they were rumbling again, announcing the last Mass.) "They're ringing for her."

"She's no longer of this world."

"God rest her soul."

And the Finizio family, as if dazed, murmured:

"On this day!"

"Who would have expected it!"

"Now we must go and offer our condolences!"

"Certainly not," Signora Finizio burst out. "It wouldn't be polite. Close them! Close the windows! God rest her soul. Let's go back inside."

Turning, she bumped into Nana, who had come toward the balcony, and now, leaning on her stick, with her puffy face upturned, all confused, raised her big eyes questioningly.

"Who was it? Who was it?"

"Donn'Amelia is dead. God bless us!" her sister shouted in her ear.

"The bread? What does she want with the bread?" answered Nana, bewildered.

"Unstop your ears, aunt," Eduardo said harshly. "They haven't brought her any bread, in fact, she'll never eat any again. She died suddenly."

"Oh, oh, oh!" said the old woman, and her horrible, crimson-colored face darkened, her eyes lowered and filled with tears. That was life, one day or the next, when youth had gone: the poorhouse or a coffin.

Anastasia needed to go to her room to get a handkerchief. Her heart that day was as delicate as the strings of a violin, and vibrated if it were merely touched. She wept, not so much out of pity for the dead woman, whom she knew and respected, as out of tenderness for this life, which appeared so strange and profound, as she had never seen it, resonant with emotion. It was as if, for some hours, she had been drinking two or three glasses of wine all at once: everything was so new, so intense in its daily simplicity. Never, ever had she been so aware of the faces, the voices of her mother, her siblings, other people. That was why her eyes were full of tears: not because Donn'Amelia was lying on her deathbed, pale-faced and meek as she had always been, but because in this life there were so many things, there was life and death, the sighs of the flesh and despair, sumptuously laid tables and dirty work, the bells of Christmas and the tranquil hills of Poggioreale. Because, while downstairs they were lighting candles, a kilometer away was the port, where Antonio's ship was anchored, and Antonio himself, who had been so dear to her, at this hour was sitting at the table, with his relatives, thinking of who knows whom or what. And suddenly she realized that, amid so many emotions, her deepest thoughts had returned to being calm, cold, inert, as they had always been, and she no longer cared about Antonio or about life itself.

She didn't wonder why this was. She sat again on the bed, as she had that morning, and, looking calmly at the plainest and most familiar details of the room—the chairs, the old paintings, the dried olive branches against the white of the walls—she was thinking what her life would be like twenty years from now. She saw herself still in this house (she didn't see her own face), she heard the slightly irritated sound of her voice calling her nephews and nieces. Everything would be like today, on that Christmas in twenty years. Only the figures changed. But what would be different? They would still be called Anna, Eduardo,

Petrillo, with the same cold faces, joyless, lifeless. They would be the same, even if in reality they had changed. Life, in their family, produced only this: a faint noise.

She was amazed, remembering the festive atmosphere of the morning, that budding of hopes, of voices. A dream, it had been: there was nothing left. Not for that reason could life be called worse. Life … it was a strange thing, life. Every so often she seemed to understand what it was, and then poof, she forgot, sleep returned.

The bell rang in the hallway, and right afterward steps could be heard, exclamations, animated voices, including Signora Finizio's, secretly victorious. "My dear lady, what a pity, have you heard?" It was the neighbor from next door, coming to borrow some coffee. On the street, which should have been deserted, two imbeciles were intently blowing into a bagpipe and because no other voice arose, no other sound, that sad and tender note spread everywhere, at times mingling with a light wind now meandering across the Neapolitan sky.

"Anastasia!" called Signora Finizio. Of course she needed something. "Anastasia!" she repeated after a moment.

Mechanically, in that torpor that had now taken over her brain and made her inert, Anastasia went to the closet, opened it, and, seeing the blue coat, which hung there like an abandoned person, delicately ran her fingers over it, feeling a compassion that wasn't, however, connected to anything, to any particular memory or suffering. Then, suddenly aware of her mother's call, she answered slowly, with no intonation:

"I'm coming."

THE GOLD OF FORCELLA

～～～

The bus that was supposed to take me to the intersection of Via Duomo and Via San Biagio dei Librai was so crowded that it was impossible for me to get off at the right stop. When I finally did set foot on the ground, I found myself staring at the dismal façade of the Central Station, along with the monument to Garibaldi, and a procession of faded green tramcars, rickety black taxis, and carriages drawn by small, sleepy horses. I turned and headed back the way I'd come until I reached Via Pietro Colletta, in the renowned Tribunali neighborhood. The sky was bright blue, as dazzling as a postcard, and beneath that luminosity people came and went in a great confusion amid buildings that rose like clouds here and there in no apparent order, and I stopped at the beginning of Via Forcella somewhat perplexed. Farther up the narrow street there was a terrific commotion, a buzz of mournful voices, and a wave of colors, red and black predominant. A market, I thought, or a street fight. An old woman was sitting near a stone at the corner and I stopped to ask her what all those people were doing. She raised her face, pitted by smallpox and framed by a large black kerchief, and took a look for herself at that distant strip of sunlight at the heart of Forcella and source of that intermittent mournful buzz, where the crowd was bulging like a snake. "*Niente stanno facenno, signò*—No one's doing nothing, signora," she said calmly, "you're dreaming."

It was years since I'd been down here, and I'd forgotten that Via Forcella, along with Via San Biagio dei Librai, is one of the most densely populated streets in Naples, where the hustle and bustle often gives one the sensation that something extraordinary must be happening. Through a veil of dust, the sun gave off a reddish glow that had lost all cheerfulness. From the thresholds of hundreds of small shops or from chairs set out along the sidewalks, women and children stared up at it with a strange, dazed air. Even the donkeys hitched to the vegetable carts seemed struck by the peculiar murkiness of the light, twitching their long ears to shoo the flies with a silent, apathetic patience. From within a small pushcart, like those used by the sanitation authority, which seemed to have been momentarily abandoned in the middle of the street, a head could be seen; beneath it was the trunk of a man of about fifty, carefully dressed in a jacket buttoned to the neck and sewn at the sides and lower hemline like a sack. A small gilt plate tied to his chest with twine invited passersby to give alms, but no one noticed him and, to be honest, he didn't do much himself to attract the public's pity. With his wine-reddened cheek resting against a sack, his ears also reddened by wine, even glowing, his white hair cascading over his eyebrows, and a delicate smile on his parted lips, the citizen slept. Meanwhile, all around him dwarves of both sexes passed by, respectably dressed in black, with pale, distorted faces, large sorrowful eyes, and twig-like fingers held at their chests, careful to avoid colliding with children and dogs. Other beggars, cripples or simply professionals, were sprawled on the ground wearing images of this or that patron saint around their necks or holding signs listing their misfortunes and their children—a sight that was replicated in the more fashionable streets of the city, in Chiaia or Piazza dei Martiri. They waited politely, or dreamed. Several church bells rang out loudly, calling these souls to Mass.

As I came out of Forcella onto Via Duomo, the traffic seemed more orderly and almost silent, but soon became even louder again in the San Biagio dei Librai district, which could be described as a continuation of Forcella.

Like other ancient, impoverished streets in Naples, Via San Biagio dei Librai was packed with shops selling gold. A lackluster glass display case, an excessively polished counter (so many ladies' elbows and hands having leaned on it for probably more than a century), a bespectacled shadow of a man who cautiously balances a shiny object in his hand and silently observes it, while a woman, young or old, standing before him at the counter, eyes him anxiously. Another scene, even more intense: the trap now momentarily empty, the same maggot, coming out onto the shop's threshold as if taking a break, looks vaguely around him, spying, in turn, in the crowd, the approach of a pale, hungry face, the eyes full of shame. That carpet of flesh which, even as I entered San Biagio dei Librai, had appeared extremely dense to me, seemed to disappear the deeper in I went, or at least it wasn't as extraordinary, much like a fresco when you move up close to it. The fact remained that, as in Forcella, I had never before seen so many beings together, walking or hanging out, colliding and fleeing one another, greeting one another from their windows and calling out from the shops, bargaining over the price of goods, or yelling out a prayer, in the same sweet, aching singers' voices that had more the tone of a lament than of the vaunted Neapolitan cheer. It was truly something that both shocked and eclipsed all one's thoughts. Most alarming was the number of children, a force perhaps sprung from the unconscious, who were not remotely supervised or blessed, as could be determined by the black halo hanging over the head of each. Every so often, one of them would emerge from a hole in the pavement, move a few steps out onto the sidewalk, and then scurry back in like a rat. The alleys off this street, itself narrow and eroded, were even narrower and more eroded. I didn't see the sheets for which Naples is well known, only the black hollows in which they were once hung: windows, doors, balconies where tin cans sprouted withered bits of lemon verbena. I felt compelled to search behind the miserable windowpanes for walls, and furnishings, and perhaps other little windows opening onto a flowering garden at the back of the house; but there was nothing to be seen except a confused jumble of various items such as blankets or the remains of baskets and vases, a chair on which a woman, like a sacred image blackened by time, sat with her yellow cheekbones jutting out, her eyes unmoving, thoughtful, black hair pinned on top of her head, sticklike arms folded in her lap. At the far end of the street, like a Persian rug worn down to clumps and threads, lay bits of the most varied kind of garbage, from amid which issued forth the pale, swollen, or bizarrely thin figures of more children, with large shaved heads and soft eyes. Few were clothed, and those who were wore shirts that exposed their bellies; almost all were barefoot or wore sandals from another era, held together with string. Some played with tin cans, others, lying on the ground, were intent on covering their faces with dust, still others seemed to be busy building a little altar with a stone and a saint, and there were those who, gracefully imitating a priest, turned to offer their blessing.

To look for their mothers would be insanity. Every so often one would dash out from behind the wheel of a carriage and, screaming at the top of her lungs, grab a child by the wrist and drag him into a lair from which emanated shouts and cries. There you might see a comb brandished, or an iron washbasin on a chair into which the unfortunate lad was forced to plunge his pitiful face.

In contrast to the savage cruelty of the alleys was the sweetness on the faces of the Madonnas with their infant Christs, of the Virgins and Martyrs, who appeared in almost every shop in San Biagio dei Librai, bent over a gilded cradle decorated with flowers and veiled with lace, not a hint of which existed in reality. It didn't take much to understand that passions here were cultish in nature and precisely for this reason had deteriorated into vice and folly; in the end, a race devoid of all logic and reason had latched on to this shapeless tumult of feelings, and humankind was now a shadow of itself, weak, neurotic, resigned to fear and impudent joy. Amorphous poverty, silent as a spider, unraveling and then reweaving in its fashion those wretched fabrics, entangling the lowest levels of the populace, which here reigned supreme. It was extraordinary to think how, instead of declining or stagnating, the population grew and, increasing, became ever more lifeless, causing drastic confusion for the local government's convictions, while the hearts of the clergy were swollen with a strange pride and even stranger hope. Here Naples was not bathed by the sea. I was sure that no one had ever seen this place or remembered it. In this dark pit only the fire of sexuality burned bright under an eerie black sky.

It was noon, and on each of the past few days it had rained precisely at that hour; accordingly, I watched the sky cover over with a layer of gauze that immediately caused the shadows of the buildings to fade, along with the already tenuous shadows of the people. Some women were walking ahead of me, preceded by a pair of very tall priests, their waxen hands grasping red leather books, who soon disappeared down an arcade with a rustle of cassocks. The women held in their hands small white packages, and every so often glanced inside them, sighing and chatting. When they arrived in front of the Church of Sant'Angelo a Nilo, they crossed themselves, then entered a courtyard opposite.

O Magnum Pietatis Opus was written across the pediment of the building at the far end of the courtyard. The lifeless gray façade resembled those of the hospitals and nursing homes in the neighborhoods of Naples. But behind this one, instead of hospital beds, there was the long line of windows of the Monte dei Pegni pawnshop, a "great charity operation" run by the Bank of Naples.

When I arrived on the third floor of the building, before one of the most majestic doors I have ever seen, groups of poor people were already there, sitting on the stairs or on their packages: pregnant women, old women, sick women, those who could no longer stand and who had begged a relative or a friend to hold their place in line. Making my way cautiously amid those bodies, I pushed open the door and found myself in an immense room with a very high ceiling, lit by two large sets of windows, like wings, on either side, and above each of those windows was another large, square, hermetically sealed window. Long spiderwebs, like thin rags, were suspended in midair.

It was the room designated for dealing in precious objects.

A vast crowd, only nominally in a line, was clamoring in front of the windows for "New Pledges." The commotion was due to the fact that on that very morning an order had come down to give as little as possible as a loan against each pawn.

Some people, their faces pale as lemons and framed by frightful permanents, turned the gray pawn tickets over and over in their hands with an air of disappointment. A very large old woman, all stomach, with bloodshot eyes, wept ostentatiously as she kissed and rekissed a chain before parting with it. Other women, and a few thin-faced men, waited calmly on a black bench set against the wall. Children wearing only shirts sat on the floor and played.

"Nunzia Apicella!" a clerk shouted from a distance, toward the small crowd redeeming their pledges. "Aspasia De Fonzo!"

Names were called by the minute but were drowned out by the fervent chatter of people commenting on the new proviso, unable to resign themselves to it. A guard with a black mustache and big, languid eyes, who wore his uniform as if it were a bathrobe, paced up and down, indifferent and bored, every so often making a show of pushing people back into orderly lines. He was speaking to someone or other when the grand door to the hall opened abruptly, and in walked a red-haired woman of around forty, dressed in black, dragging two extraordinarily pale children behind her. That unhappy woman, who was later revealed to be one Antonietta De Liguoro, *zagrellara*, or haberdasher, had learned on the street that the bank where she was heading to pawn a chain was closing early that day and wouldn't let her in. With her flushed red face and her blue eyes nearly out of their sockets, she begged everyone to do her a favor since she needed to pawn her chain before closing so that her husband could depart for Turin where their oldest son was gravely ill. Nothing could calm her. Even when she had been assured that she could certainly get in line, she continued to sob and cry:

"*Mamma del Carmine*, Mother of God, help me."

Many of the women, forgetting their own great sorrow of

moments earlier, took up her cause. Those farther away called out heartfelt messages of encouragement and blessings. Those nearer touched her shoulders and hands, used their own hairpins to fix her hair, not to mention the attention showered on the two children, the prolonged and theatrical cries of "Mamma's darlings." The two creatures, who were perhaps three and four, skinny and pale as worms, wore on their waxen faces little smiles so wizened and cynical that it was a marvel to see, and every once in a while they gave their frenzied mother the once-over with a mischievous and questioning air. A kind of uprising immediately transported the woman, whose trials and tribulations everyone now knew, up to the window, leapfrogging the ferocious bureaucracy of waiting one's turn. And here is the mesmerizing conversation I overheard:

Clerk (after having examined the chain, dryly): Three thousand eight hundred lire.

Zagrellara: *Facìte quattromila, sì*—Come on, make it four thousand, won't you?

Clerk: Take it or leave it, my dear.

Zagrellara: But my husband's got to take the train, I swear it, we have a sick son as well as these two little rascals ... do it for love of the Madonna!

Clerk (very calmly): Three thousand eight hundred ... up to you ... (and turning to another clerk): Amedeo, ask Salvatore, *purtasse n'atu cafè*—bring me another cup of coffee, will you? ... No sugar.

Her eyes still bloodshot, but now perfectly dry, Antonietta De Liguoro retraced her steps of moments earlier, proudly ignoring, or perhaps truly not seeing because of her grief, those who had earlier rallied around her with their Christian pity. She seemed not even to notice the two children following behind her, their little hands gripping her dress.

"That one there," the guard said to a young man who looked like a student, a red briefcase under his arm with the edge of a towel sticking out, "has been talking about her husband taking a train to Turin for a year. *Nun tene nisciuno*—there's no one in Turin, no husband, either. *Nun vo' 'a fila ... e i' nun 'a dico niente*—she don't want to wait in line, and I won't say anything." His gaze followed the cunning *zagrellara*, who, after pausing briefly at the cashier's desk, was now hurrying toward the door with the money and a gray pawn ticket pressed tightly to her chest. Miserable and compassionate, the crowd forgot itself in order to attend to the presumed victim with words of comfort and indignation in the face of an age-old injustice that had by now seeped into everyone. "Jesus Christ will console her ... Mamma del Carmine will help her ... God rubs salt in the wound," and stares of deep hatred were aimed at the bank windows and at the ceiling, where all could see the local authorities and the government promenading among the spiderwebs.

Meanwhile, a clerk's indifferent voice had resumed calling out: "Di Vincenzo, Maria; Fusco, Addolorata ... ; Della Morte, Carmela ..."

All of a sudden, there was a great silence, then a murmur of astonishment, of childish surprise, ran through the three lines waiting in front of the New Pledges windows.

"What's the matter with you?" asked the clerk, peering out his window, but no one paid any attention. Somehow or other, a brown butterfly with a profusion of tiny gold stripes on its wings and back had entered through the door leading to the stairs and was flying over that melee of heads, hunched shoulders, and anxious stares; now it fluttered ... rose up ... dove down ... happy ... careless, never making up its mind to land in one place.

"Oh! ... Oh! ... Oh! ..." murmured the crowd.

"*O' bbi lloco 'o ciardino!*—There, look at the garden!" a woman said to her newborn, who was crying softly, his head on her shoulder. Near the door an old crippled woman, her mouth full of bread, was singing.

THE INVOLUNTARY CITY

One of the things to see in Naples—after the requisite visits to the excavations of Pompeii, to the dormant Solfatara volcano, and, if there is time, the Vesuvian crater—is the building known as Granili III and IV* in the coastal neighborhood that connects the port to the first suburbs on Vesuvius. It is around three hundred meters long, between fifteen and twenty meters wide, and a lot taller. To someone who sees it unexpectedly, getting off one of the small trams operating along the workers' routes, it looks like a hill or a bald mountain, invaded by termites, which traverse it with no sound or sign that reveals a particular purpose. In the past, the walls were a dark red, which still emerges, here and there, amid vast patches of yellow and dabs of an equivocal green. I could count a hundred and seventy-four openings, the majority of them barred, on the single façade which is of an unprecedented width and height for modern taste; some terraces; and, at the back of the building, eight sewage pipes that,

---

* Originally built as a granary in the 18th century, this vast seafront structure later became a barracks and was bombed in 1943. Despite heavy damage, huge numbers of Neapolitans left homeless in World War II took refuge in the complex. It was demolished soon after Ortese's book first appeared in 1953 and its occupants were transferred to public housing on the outskirts of Naples.

situated on the third floor, let their slow waters flow along the silent wall. There are three floors, plus a ground floor, half hidden in the earth and protected by a ditch, and they contain three hundred and forty-eight rooms, all equally high and large, distributed with perfect regularity to the right and left of four corridors, one per floor, whose total length is one kilometer two hundred meters. Every corridor is illuminated by no more than twenty-eight lamps, each with five candlepower. The width of each corridor is from seven to eight meters, and so the word "corridor" designates, more than anything else, four streets of an ordinary city neighborhood, elevated like the floors of a bus, and without any sky. Especially for the ground floor and the two floors above it, the light of the sun is represented by those twenty-eight electric lamps, which here shine weakly both day and night.

On the two sides of each corridor eighty-six doors of private dwellings open, forty-three on the right, forty-three on the left (plus that of a bathroom), marked by a series of numbers that go from one to three hundred and forty-eight. In each of these spaces between one and five families live, with an average of three families per room. The total number of inhabitants of this dwelling is three thousand people, divided into five hundred and seventy families, with an average of six people per family. When three, four, or five families live in the same space, it reaches a density of twenty-five or thirty inhabitants per room.

Having stated in summary fashion some facts about the structure and population of this Neapolitan neighborhood, one realizes that one has expressed almost nothing. Every day, in a thousand expert offices in all the cities and countries of the globe, perfect machines line up numbers and sums of statistics, intended to precisely describe how and in what measure the economic, political, and moral life of every single community and nation originates, grows, and dissolves. Other data, of an almost astral depth, refer instead to the life and nature of ancient peoples, their system of rule, triumphs, civilization, and demise; or, skipping over every historical interest dear to our hearts, address themselves to life or the probability of life on the planets that shine in space. Granili III and IV, one of the most evocative phenomena in the world, and like Southern Italy, dead to the progress of time, should therefore be, rather than described with ingenuous figures by this or that obscure reporter, visited carefully, in all its deformities and absurd horror, by groups of economists, jurists, doctors. Special commissions could go and count the number of living and dead, and of the former and the latter examine the reasons that led them there or kept them there or carried them away, because Granili III and IV is not only what could be called a temporary settlement of homeless people but, rather, the demonstration, in clinical and legal terms, of the fall of a race. According to the most charitable judgment, only a profoundly diseased human system could tolerate, as Naples tolerates, without being disturbed, the putrefaction of one of its limbs, because this, and no other, is the sign under which the institution of the Granili lives and thrives. To seek in Naples the nadir of Naples no longer occurs to anyone after a visit to the Bourbon barracks. Here the barometers no longer display any measure; compasses go crazy. The men you meet can't do you any harm: ghosts from a life in which wind and sun existed— these good things they no longer remember. They creep or climb or stagger: that is their way of moving. They speak very little; they are no longer Neapolitans, or anything else. A committee of priests and American scholars, which, days ago, boldly crossed the threshold of that melancholy dwelling, quickly turned back, with incoherent words and looks.

I had marked on a box of matches, which was later useful for other reasons, the name of Signora Antonia Lo Savio. One morning in November, with no other direction, I crossed the threshold of the grand entrance that opens on the right side of Granili III and IV. The porter, sitting behind a large black caldron in which clothes were boiling, examined me coldly, and when she told me that she didn't know who this Lo Savio was, and that I should go and ask on the first floor, I felt the temptation to put it all off to another day. It was a violent temptation, like nausea in the face of surgery. Behind me, in the area in front of the building, a dozen children were playing, almost without speaking, throwing stones. Some, seeing me, had stopped playing, and approached silently. In front of me, I saw the ground-floor corridor, extending for three hundred meters, but at that moment it seemed an incalculable distance. In the center and toward the end of this conduit some shadows moved, without any precision, like molecules in a beam of light; some small fires gleamed; from behind one of the doors came a persistent, harsh lullaby. Gusts of a bitter odor, mainly of toilets, continually reached the threshold, mixed with the darker smell of dampness. It seemed impossible to advance ten meters into that tunnel without fainting. Taking a few steps, I saw a dim light to my right, and discovered one of those stairways with very wide steps, no higher than a finger, which once allowed horses, kept on the ground floor, to reach the first floor with their burdens. Maybe it was less cold than I had feared, but the darkness was almost absolute. I risked stumbling, and I lighted a match, but immediately extinguished it: here were some very small lamps, inside which reddish wires quivered and writhed continuously. In this glimmer, the first-floor corridor took shape.

Toward the end, someone was roasting coffee, adding burned beans to the smell of urine and dampness. The smoke, however, made one's eyes tear, and put a pinker halo around the lights, tiny as pins. I passed a group of children, seeing them only when they were close to me; they were playing ring-around-the-rosy, holding one another by the hand but at a distance, and throwing back their disheveled heads, with a pleasure stronger than that of a normal game. I grazed locks of hard hair, as if pasted, and arms whose flesh was cold. Finally I saw the woman who was roasting the coffee, sitting in the doorway of her home. Inside there was a disorder and a savage glow, from an unexpected ray of sunlight that fell from the window (open at the back of the building), amid pots and rags, onto the mattresses. There was also some blood. The woman, dark and lean, was sitting on a chair that had lost its straw seat, and, with a kind of pride, kept turning the wooden handle of the iron cylinder, from whose little door rose a cloud of smoke, surrounding her head. Three or four other girls, in black dresses open over white chests, stood near her, and followed with bright, serious eyes the dance of the beans in the cylinder. Seeing me, they moved aside, and the woman stopped bouncing the cylinder on the fire, which for a moment almost ceased to provide any light. The name Antonia Lo Savio left them silent. I realized later, during subsequent visits, that that silence, rather than indicating puzzlement or indecision, manifested curiosity and a more sinister, if weak, feeling: the desire to drag, for a moment, into the obscurity in which they dominated, the stranger who was obviously habituated to light. At least, during my visits, many of these people seemed to enjoy not answering me or directing me to places from which I would not easily have been able to get out. I was about to keep going, making an effort to appear calm, when one of the girls, turning toward a door, said slowly in dialect, without looking at me: "*Vidite lloco*—You're looking at the place."

A small woman, completely bloated, like a dying bird, her black hair cascading over a hunchback, and with a lemon-colored face, dominated by a large, pointed nose that hung over a harelip, was combing her hair in front of a fragment of mirror, holding some hairpins between her teeth. She smiled, seeing me, and said, "*Nu minuto*—just a minute." My happiness at seeing such a smile in such a place led me to reflect for a moment whether it was fitting or not to address her as "signora." She was only an enormous flea, but what grace and kindness animated her tiny eyes. "Signora," I said, approaching rapidly, and I mentioned the name of Dr. De Luca, the director of the clinic for the poor of the Granili, who had sent me to her so that she could show me around a bit. "*Nu minuto* ... if you will be so kind as to oblige me," she repeated, continuing to smile and comb her hair, and I noticed then that, behind the rattle of catarrh, her voice was sweet. I think it was that sensation, unconsciously perceived, that somewhat restored my courage. I leaned against the door, waiting for that creature to finish combing her hair, and meanwhile I glanced at the coffee roasters. The smoke had thinned and in that sudden gray they appeared even paler. They murmured a few words, in which the name of Signora Lo Savio figured, with a silent laugh, full of disdain, and I was disturbed by what I thought were the reasons for that hostility. Signora Lo Savio, in the doorway of her home, was finishing with her hair, with a certain girlish delay, as if it were May and she were thinking of her love, when a child, hands in pockets, hair straight on his head, with a bold yet dark expression, approached. He proceeded, with an imperceptible hesitation, toward the center of the room, and went to sit on the bed platform (I never saw, in this great structure, a made bed, only mattresses spread out or piled up, at most with a covering thrown on top). Once seated, and swinging his thin legs, he began to sing softly: "*E ce steva 'na vota 'na reggina, che teneva i capille anella anella*—Once upon a time there was a queen who had curly curly hair," in a toneless voice. He broke off suddenly to speak to Signora Lo Savio—"Signora, do you have a little bread?"—and from this I understood that she wasn't his relative. While Signora Lo Savio, with the last hairpin in her mouth, answered something, I approached the child and asked him his name. He answered, "Luigino." I asked other questions and he didn't respond at all. On his whole face appeared an ambiguous, disdainful smile, which contrasted bizarrely with the dead, absent expression of his eyes. Feeling embarrassed, as if his smile, mysteriously mature, already the smile not of a child but of a man, and of a man accustomed to dealing only with prostitutes, contained a judgment, an atrocious evaluation of my person, I moved a few steps away. And here was Signora Lo Savio approaching with the bread, which the boy began to eat. "That poor child," she now said, "has neither father nor mother. He's been here since '46, with a cousin of mine, next door. On top of that, he's also blind."

The boy was silent for a moment, and in that moment the hands that clutched the bread slid down to his knees. In some way he was observing me. "I see a little; and now I see a shadow lowering its head. Are you going, signora?"

I answered yes, after a few moments, and set off with Signora Lo Savio.

"I'd come with you but I'm waiting for a friend," he continued, with a new intonation, in which the boldness of the lie, necessary to save him, died in a kind of stunned piety, a tender warmth. He had raised his head for a moment and, laying it back down on the straw, he began singing again, "*E 'na barca arrivaie alla marina*—and a boat arrived at the port" in a faint voice and with a steadiness that must have had the purpose, every morning, of cajoling him again to sleep.

Coming out with my guide, I sought in my confused mind reasons that would allow me to immediately abandon that place, and reach the square and the first bus or tram stop. It seemed to me that, as soon as I was out of there, I would shout and run to hug the first people I encountered. I looked at Signora Lo Savio, but my eyes kept moving away from her. I didn't quite know where to place them. In the light of the few lamps, I saw her better: queen of the house of the dead, a crushed figure, bloated, horrendous, the fruit, in her turn, of profoundly defective creatures, and yet something regal remained in her: a confidence in the way she moved and spoke, and something else, as well—a vivid flash in the depths of her mouse-like eyes, in which one could surely perceive, along with the knowledge of evil and its extent, all the human pleasure needed to confront it. Behind that deplorable forehead, a measure of hope existed. Having realized that I was stumbling as I walked, she hurried to guide my elbow with her hand, but without touching it. This persistence of humility amid such unremitting courage, this dignity in keeping her distance from those whom she considered saved, imposed on me a certain calm, and I said to myself that I had no right to appear weak. We walked along the corridor of the first floor, toward the horse stairs, leading to the ground floor, which, according to my guide, was the most important thing. In a few words, she explained to me the reason for the aversion of a good part of the female population of the place. It had begun when Signora Lo Savio decided to devote herself to the clinic, and was then suspected of enjoying the partiality of the director, and of gaining immediate advantages from her activity, like medicines, that she would resell, food packages from the local welfare agency, and other things. "Six months ago I abandoned my home and everything," she confessed simply. "I comb my hair and I come down. Because this is not a home, signora, you see, this is a place of afflictions. Wherever you pass, the walls groan."

It wasn't the walls, of course, it was the wind, which crept in between the great doors; the big structure really seemed to be shuddering continuously, almost imperceptibly, as if from an internal landslide, from an anguish and dissolution of all the quasi-human material that composed it. Now the walls appeared wet, corroded, all encrustations and dark drips. We met two children going up, chasing each other with obscene gestures. A woman came down from the second floor, carrying a green bottle wrapped in a handkerchief, as if it were a child, and with her other hand pressing her cheek, from which a kind of lump of reddish fungus protruded, perhaps caused by the dampness. Suddenly, we heard a breathless, very strange voice singing a sacred hymn in which the goodness of existence was praised. "That's the maestro," said Signora Lo Savio, "a holy man, a refined person. He's had asthma for twenty-five years, and he can't work anymore. But when he feels better, he always talks about God."

I thought that the door she pushed was that of the asthmatic. We were on the ground floor, and the darkness and the silence were slightly more intense than before, broken only by the vague gray glow that appeared in the distance, three hundred meters away, where the corridor ended, and by the imperceptible lamps that followed one another like fireflies attached to the ceiling. Here and there, doors, doors, doors, but made of boards, or metal sheets, or sometimes even pieces of cardboard or faded curtains.

"May I?"

"Please."

Strange room. A woman in the background, enormous and strong, dressed in black, upright behind a table, was smoking a butt. On the table stood an empty bottle and a wooden spoon. Behind the woman, like a curtain, was an immense window, with some boards nailed to it and crisscrossed by stakes, in such a way as to impede the passage of the slightest bit of light or air. In this room, that is, 258B, there was a persistent odor of feces, collected in hidden chamber pots, the same that we found in almost all these rooms. These chamber pots must have been placed behind partitions composed of packing paper or shreds of blankets, and no more than a meter high, which divided the space into two or three lodgings. The woman had immediately looked at my hands, with a dark eye, made shifty by a squint, and seeing that they were empty displayed an expression of disappointment. Because the ladies of the Neapolitan aristocracy from time to time send packages, the stranger who arrives here empty-handed can be considered only an enemy or a lunatic. I understood this slowly.

"This lady," Signora Lo Savio said, "has come to see how you are. She can be useful to you. Talk to her, talk, my dear."

That mean, squinting gaze fell on me still, descending down my neck like a sticky liquid. Then, overcoming the weight and weariness of the enormous flesh that enfolded her, Maria De Angelis said, in a whining, unpleasant voice that was as if charged with disgust but also clouded by a deep sleep: "Help us."

At the foot of a mattress on the floor, there were some crusts of bread, and amid these, barely moving, like dust balls, three long sewer rats were gnawing on the bread. The woman's voice was so normal, in its weary disgust, and the scene so tranquil, and those three animals appeared so sure of being able to gnaw on those crusts of bread, that I had the impression that I was dreaming, or at least contemplating a drawing, of a horrendous truthfulness, that had mesmerized me to the point of making me confuse a representation with life itself. I knew that those animals would soon go back into their hole, as in fact, after a few moments, they did, but now the whole room was infected by them, along with the woman in black, and Signora Lo Savio and I myself: it seemed to me that we partook of their dark nature. Meanwhile from behind a curtain came a youth in evening dress, adjusting his tie, his face covered by pustules, and skin, under those brown spots, of a pale green. He had a violin in his hand, and just touched it with his old fingers.

"My son, a street musician," the mother introduced him.

"Do you earn something?"

"Depends."

"Do you have other children?" I said to the mother.

"With this one, seven. Antonio, boot cleaner; Giuseppe, porter; this one who plays; one mentally ill; the others unemployed."

"And your husband?"

She didn't answer.

As we went out, a youth dressed almost like a woman, with a shawl over his shoulders and a delicate appearance, greeted me, bowing to the floor. "Oh, Ma," I heard him say as he entered the house, turning to the woman, "today I saw a little house near the sea, there was lemon verbena growing, I'd like to rent it." He said other confused words, then he returned to the doorway, making faces, with a thoughtful air.

Maestro Cutolo's house was a few meters farther on, opposite that of the lunatic, and I realized why that good man sang. A benefactor who hadn't wanted to give his name had made a gift to the teacher, providing some glass panes that had been installed in the high window. Thus flooded with the pale winter light, the big room appeared clean and in a certain way cheerful, an impression that wasn't later refuted. Sitting on the floor in the sun, two lovely children were playing; they were almost naked, with black slanting eyes and serious smiles. Signor Cutolo, who opened the door, was in his underwear, and he apologized profusely for this detail. We had pleasantly surprised him with our visit, and he hadn't had time to straighten himself. He was a man still young, around forty, of medium height, but so slender as to seem an adolescent. His hair was blond, his eyes blue, his face hollow and flooded by a smile whose depths, like the bottom of a shallow pool, were an inconsolable sadness. "I'm happy," he declared to us immediately, "because my heart is full of holy obedience to God's wishes."

"Do you feel better today?" my guide asked. "We overheard you singing."

"Thanks to the holy indulgence of God to his poor servant, yes," he answered politely, breathless.

I looked at him, and that face seemed to remind me of another, like an old image veiled by a new one. Suddenly, I found again the man he had been twenty years earlier, when I lived in a building in the Naples port zone which at that time was full of commerce, flags, sails, cargoes, and the joy of money. He, Cutolo, was an office boy at the Compagnia di Navigazione Garibaldi, on the third floor. He hurried to church whenever he could; he was from a respectable family and had an accountant's diploma.

"How ever did you get here?"

"During the war, my home was destroyed. My father died, God bless his soul, and it was left to me to support my mother and two sisters. The holy will of God decided that this sacrifice would not last long. God called my mother to him; one sister married a soldier, and now is in Avellino; another lives in Sezione Avvocata, with a widow. I, thank God, now I have my little home, my children, a good wife, I can't complain. The clinic gives me medicines."

"What does your wife do?"

"Maid, with a devout family."

His eyes sunken by the effort to breathe, he looked at me and smiled.

"I eat medicine, I eat it. I'm ashamed of taking such great advantage of Dr. De Luca's kindness."

He called the children, who approached slowly, and held them close by his side, with a flash of inexpressible pride. They were naked, and their beautiful faces, their gazes, were healthy and yet sad. I imagined their mother, a strong peasant, a servant.

"For the Holy Year I would have liked another one, my wife didn't obey," he said with sweet vanity. "She refused the Creator Spirit who animates the world."

The two brothers stared first at me, then at him, with thoughtful faces, biting their dirty nails.

"I love children so much, there would be so much to do here," Cutolo continued, with anxious sadness, looking toward the door. "In this house there must be at least eight hundred of these kids, but they are unacquainted with holy obedience: unfortunately they haven't been brought up well. Sometimes I call them, I'd like to teach them the principles of our holy religion, some inspirational songs, like this, to improve them. But they refuse, they always refuse."

As he spoke, the heads of some individuals between seven and ten years of age peeked in through the door, which had been left open. A dozen attentive eyes, some red and half closed, some full of an animal greed, rolled in deep sockets. One of them, who had a particularly strong, intelligent face, clutched something in his hand. Suddenly, one of the little Cutolo brothers began to shout and jump up and down like a lunatic, holding one foot in his hand: *"Oi ma,' Oi ma.'"* He had been hit with a stone, and, at the same time, as silently as they had appeared, those four or five figures disappeared.

The teacher, after a moment of hesitation, perhaps of shame, began to comfort his son, urging him to forgive those rascals who had not had the advantage of a Christian education. Coming out the door, I saw the boys, who had stopped in the darkness, twenty meters on, breathing hard, like the teacher, with the same expression of ineffable joy in their eyes.

Although I had seen only these few things, it was late. In the city and elsewhere, in the whole world, it was time for people to go home. Even here, in this land of night, some were returning, groping their way from the end of the corridor, tramps, beggars, musicians, faceless men and women. In a few homes someone was cooking: smoke, which had the density of a blue body, escaped from some doors, yellow flames could be glimpsed inside, the black faces of people squatting, holding a bowl on their knees. In other rooms, instead, everything was motionless, as if life had become petrified; men still in bed turned under gray blankets, women were absorbed in combing their hair, in the enchanted slow motion of those who do not know what will be, afterward, the other occupation of their day. The entire ground floor, and the first floor to which we were ascending, were in these conditions of depressed inertia. One expected nothing, and no one. On the second and third floors, Signora Lo Savio explained to me, life assumed instead a human aspect, resumed a rhythm that might in some way resemble that of a normal city. The women made the beds in the morning, they swept, dusted, tidied themselves and the children, many of whom were sent off, with real black smocks and blue ties, to a school run by the nuns. A number of the men had jobs. They'd acquired radios and had those sewage pipes constructed, which, set up on the third floor, afflicted the inhabitants on the lower floors with their stink and stained their windows.

While we went up, enjoying a certain light of day that began to pour down from the staircase, and breathing a less oppressive air, we were joined by a group of boys and girls in their black smocks, with bows and schoolbags, who were returning from school. Through an open door, a radio was broadcasting. We heard a clear male voice, the announcer of Radio Roma, utter: "And now, dear listeners," and shortly afterward the voice of a singer modulated the first notes of Passion. As in all Naples, here, too, the volume was kept very high, partly out of eagerness for the sound, a characteristic of this population, but also out of the completely bourgeois pleasure of being able to demonstrate to the neighbors that one is well off and can afford the luxury of a powerful gadget.

We didn't go into any of these homes: the families were fairly ordinary, the same you would meet on the top floors of old apartment buildings in the city. Many of the windows had been supplied with glass panes, but where they remained closed up, electric lights hung from the ceiling—lights that were definitely stronger than those on the first floors. Here one could see clearly, and, Signora Lo Savio told me, the third floor was ablaze with lights, even near the beds, which had their sheets; there were closets with regular hooks for clothes, you could see polished tables with doilies, artificial flowers, portraits, and occasionally under the wall clocks, couches. Some of the men in these families had well-paid jobs; they were white-collar employees, clerks in banks or salesclerks, good people, who were still dignified and calm, and, having lost their home after a collapse or an evacuation, and unable to find another right away, had adapted to living at the Granili, without giving up their decorum, the product of an honored tradition. They avoided any contact with the inhabitants of the first floors, demonstrating toward their degradation a severity not without compassion, and mixed with satisfaction for their own prosperity, which they attributed to a virtuous life, having no doubt with regard to its stability. At times, owing to an absolutely random circumstance, a chance event, which would soon, just as randomly, be over, like unemployment, or an illness, it happened that one of these good citizens was forced to give up his lodging, for a small sum, to a more fortunate family head, and adapt to settling with his family on a lower floor, though he was quite sure that in just a short time he would move back up to the third floor, or even leave the Granili. That man, that family, never returned to the surface, nor did they get out of there entirely, although in the first days it had seemed possible. The children, once tidy and serene, in that darkness became covered with insects and their faces grew graver and paler, the girls went with married men, the men got sick. No one rose again, from down there. It wasn't easy to climb back up those stairs that appeared so flat and accessible. There was something that called, from down there, and those who began to descend were lost, but they didn't realize it until the end.

"Signora, excuse me," a kind of *maîtresse* in a dressing gown was saying, standing in front of the door of one of these homes, with a cup in her hand and a smile in her bluish eyes. "I need some salt. I just put in the pasta, and I realized we don't have any."

Two twenty-year-old youths went back into their home, discussing the soccer game.

An old pensioner, sitting on a chair in front of his door, was reading *Il Mattino*.

Clear voices of children could be heard shouting over their soup.

In another apartment, two girls, as tall as horses, in blue sweaters, their faces powdered, were intently reading an illustrated weekly in front of the radio. *Più forte 'e 'na catena*—Stronger than a chain, cried the radio, as in all the neighborhoods of monarchic, scheming Naples, on Sundays, around one o'clock, when the ancient, familiar odor of ragù spreads through the orderly, bright rooms, full of relatives and youths returning from Mass.

We were, or at least I was, in that state of mind between anguish and relief of someone who, coming out of a prison, returns to light, air, and, in some sense, a kind of sweet human freedom, a certain standard of life, when a confused and sorrowful sound, whose meaning couldn't be clearly perceived, and which wavered between suffering and a sort of tortured relief, attracted our attention. That sound, a combination of footsteps and sobbing, rose from one of the lower floors, through the deep stairwell, which in the meantime we had again approached. The cheerful voice of the Radio Roma announcer wasn't enough to muffle it, nor was the almost serene atmosphere of the third floor.

Signora Lo Savio, after a moment of reflection, had begun to go rapidly down the stairs, without paying any attention to me, and I followed. At the second floor, with night returning, those sounds and voices were clearer: footsteps of men and women, not many, but certainly a good number, who were walking, carrying *something*, and tranquil voices that mourned or consoled. The woman whose face was covered by a fungus passed in front of us, speaking softly to a fat woman, and saying, "Now it's day, for that creature, now he'll see God!" to which the other assented placidly, drying her eyes with a rag. Other people looked out, motionless, from the doors on the corridor, commenting on the event in their dialect: "*Pazzianno è fernuto*—while he was playing he died." On the ground floor, finally, we saw what was going on. They were carrying away a certain Antonio Esposito, seven years old, nicknamed Scarpetella, who had died half an hour earlier, of unknown causes, while he was playing with some boys of his own age. Suddenly he had brought his hand to his heart and sat down in a corner. Now they were carrying him to the morgue for verification, and parents and friends were taking advantage of this to improvise a funeral. And it was, understandably, the simplest funeral I'd ever seen. The dead boy wasn't even in a coffin but in the arms of his mother, who was a yellow thing, somewhere between a fox and a trash bin. The child was half wrapped in a blanket, from which the edges hung down here and there, along with his slender arms. He was fair-haired, with a delicate face, his lips half parted in an expression of wonder, which not even the bandage around his jaws could contain. His calm and his joy, characteristic of those who have left life, were somehow emphasized by a glob of snot under his right nostril which made one think of an abandon and a silence that no one would any longer disturb. Behind them came the father, who, probably owing to some confusion in his mind at this sudden misfortune, was carrying the boy's shoes. He spoke with the priest, who was near him; he was an obese, apathetic man, making an effort to appear calm, to judge from the way he pulled the lapels of his jacket over his bare chest toward his neck. God had punished them—the year before, too, one had died like that. After the misfortune of Vincenzina they had had no peace. This one seemed sound, in good health. Behind the parents, five or six youths followed, with half-witted looks, all children of the fox and siblings of the dead child, flanked by a group of women who were praying aloud, and this, along with the false sobs of one of the brothers, was the absurd noise that had struck me. How absurd was the composure of the man and the woman, in a city like Naples, where people are constantly performing. All the doors, as on the first floor, now were open, without, however, a word spoken, not a pitiful comment, as would be customary among the lower classes. We also saw Maestro Cutolo, with his children close by his side, wearing an ecstatic expression. "A beautiful creature," he exclaimed, seeing us, "God, in His infinite goodness, wanted to take him away from all occasions for evil in this life, calling him to Himself. Let us praise His infinite wisdom. Now that little scamp Scarpetella is climbing the trees in Heaven."

He hadn't finished speaking when under those black vaults a choked, tortured, horrible cry sounded, as if the person who had produced it couldn't get free of it. At the same time, a glossy young woman of perhaps twenty, adorned with baubles, came running from the entrance to the corridor, where some light appeared. Tearing herself away from two men who accompanied her and who appeared hesitant, she ran toward the group, and for a moment mingled with it. The funeral paused, like a procession when one of the devout wants to pin an offering of money to the Madonna's robe. "What's this! You're making fun! You're heartless!" We heard no more.

"Get out!" cried a harsh voice after a moment. It was the mother, who, after the first moment of bewilderment, was trying to tear the dead child from the girl's embrace. But she, like one demented, held tight to him; practically falling to her knees, out of weakness or for some other reason, she tried to pull him to herself, and since she couldn't reach his face, as the mother tried to cover it, she embraced his bare, dirty legs, his bare feet.

"Shameless! That girl is shameless," the father now said to the priest, "she left home without a thought for us. We asked her for help in our need, and she answered that she no longer had parents. Now she's in a state because of her poor brother."

"Scarpatella!" the girl called out, with a cry in which tenderness and fear were a single thing, "Don't fool around, wake up. You called me morning and night, even in sleep. I don't have anyone, dear heart." And then out came a great wail.

Now the fox looked at her oldest daughter, with a flash, an indefinable smile, between foolish and bitter, in her shining eyes. "He was always running after her," she explained, "tap tap, in his little shoes. Now where is she? he asked when she went away."

"Have mercy," said the priest, indifferently, "God will have mercy on your poor Antonio, who at this hour stands before Him, with his little sins." He leaned over to murmur something in the ear of the young woman, who immediately looked up, with a spellbound expression, while she continued to hug to her breast the rigid bundle. She laid this down, with a kiss, in the arms of the woman, and, red in the face but with no more tears, searched in her shiny leather purse, which had slid to the ground, for a large pink bill, and handed it to the mother. She smiled, and the father, too, softened, lowering his head. The child's mouth had fallen open, and someone adjusted the bandage. Then, with the sad prayers that had made such an impression on us, the procession resumed its tranquil and apparently sorrowful journey, toward the gray arc of light that announced the way out.

After that, I didn't understand or see anything precise. Signora Lo Savio led me from door to door throughout the whole first floor, and again on the ground floor, where we had forgotten some families. Of the mournful event no one spoke, and I realized that down there no possibility of emotion survived. There was darkness, and nothing else. Silence, swift memories of another life, a sweeter life, nothing else. Not even Signora Lo Savio spoke. She would push on a door politely: "May we?" Some answered, "Come in." Some didn't answer at all; then she went in, looking around with her penetrating eyes. Immediately eight, ten, fifteen people came out of the shadows, one rising from a bed, like a dead person who is dreaming, another holding his savage head above a wooden partition for a moment. Women, whose femininity was revealed only by a skirt and hair—more like a crust of dust than a hair style—approached in silence, pushing their children in front of them, as if that cursed childhood could protect or give them heart. The men, instead, stayed behind, as if ashamed. Some looked at my shoes, my hands, not daring to raise their eyes to my face. In many families, as in that of Maria De Angelis, there was one who was introduced as mentally ill: "What work do you do?" I asked and he, after a hesitation, trying to smile: "Mentally ill." "You see!" the women cried, with a kind of triumph, "Jesus Christ wants to test us. Christ will reward those who are good to us!" And they observed Signora Lo Savio and me, anxious to hear a mention of packages. I looked mainly at the children, and realized that they could die suddenly, running around, like Scarpetella. That childhood had nothing childish about it but the number of years. Otherwise, they were little men and women, already knowing everything, the beginning and the end of things, already consumed by vices, by idleness, by the most unendurable poverty, ill in body and twisted in mind, with corrupt or foolish smiles, sly and desolate at the same time. Ninety per cent of them, Signora Lo Savio said to me, already have tuberculosis or are susceptible to it, have rickets, or are infected with syphilis, like their fathers and mothers. They are normally present when their parents copulate, and they imitate it in games. There are no other games here, apart from throwing stones. "I want to show you a little creature," she said.

She led me to the end of the hall, where, from a faint green light that was visible through a crack, one understood that evening had descended in Naples. There was a door from which came not a sound or a voice. Signora Lo Savio knocked lightly and entered without waiting for an answer, like someone who is at home.

It was a vast, clean, deserted room, somewhere between a cave and a temple. If not for the presence of a tiny lamp, whose light, placed high up, gave more irritation than joy, that place would have made you think of an ancient and forgotten ruin. There was an odor of dampness, stronger and grimmer than elsewhere, filtered by things in decay. A woman still young, and with an ecstatic look, came toward us.

"How is your Nunzia?" asked Signora Lo Savio.

"Come."

She led us to a cradle made out of a Coca-Cola carton,

which looked small and wretched against the background of one of the usual solemn, hermetically barred windows. In that little bed, without any underwear, on a very small pillow, under a hard, crusted man's jacket, rested what seemed to be a newborn with a bizarrely gentle and adultlike face: a delicate, very white face, illuminated by eyes in which the blue of evening shone, intelligent and sweet, and which moved here and there, observing everything, with an attention greater than what a child of a few months can conceive. Seeing us, those eyes rested on us, on me, rose to the forehead, turned, sought the mother, as if questioning. The mother picked up the jacket with one hand, and we saw a tiny body, the length of a few handbreadths, perfectly skeletal: the bones were as thin as pencils, the feet all wrinkles, tiny as the claws of a bird. At the contact with the cold air, the child drew them to herself, slowly. The mother let the jacket-blanket fall back.

I wasn't wrong when, seeing her, I felt that Nunzia Faiella had already known life for some time, and saw and understood everything, without being able to speak.

"That child is two years old," Signora Lo Savio whispered to me. "Because of her *internal organs*, she hasn't grown ... Nunzia, dear one ..." she called her, sadly.

Hearing those words, that being smiled weakly.

"Once I took her out ... to the doctor," said the young woman, speaking in a rough, masculine voice, between exalted and resigned (and so I understood that only once in her existence had Nunzia Faiella seen the light of the sun, perhaps a pale winter sun), "she saw the air, the sun ... she was stupefied."

Even now, Nunzia Faiella was amazed: her sweet eyes examined from time to time the high ceiling, the greenish walls, they withdrew and returned continually to the glimmer of the lamp, which perhaps reminded her of something. There was no sadness or even suffering in those eyes, in that lonely life, but a sense of waiting, of a punishment served in silence, of a thing that could come from beyond those immense walls, from beyond that high blind window, that darkness, that stench, that scent of death.

"Nunzia," Signora Lo Savio called again, bending over the carton and speaking affectionately to the creature, "what are you doing? Do you want to leave your mamma? Do you want to have Christmas with Baby Jesus?"

Then something happened that I would never have expected. The child turned to look at her mother, with an uncertain smile, which suddenly became a frown, then yielded to a weeping so weak, suffocated, and faint that it seemed to come from inside a cabinet; it was like someone crying to himself, with neither the strength nor the hope of being heard.

Coming out of that room, I collided violently with two women who had learned of the arrival of a group of journalists, and were rushing to make a complaint about an *abomination* that they had endured for some time. One of the two toilets on the ground floor had been closed on purpose, they said, and they, who were neighbors, had to go three hundred meters every day in order to empty the chamber pots into the toilet at the other end of the corridor, where the clinic was. From anger they moved on to complaint. They were tigers who had suffered too much in their life, so that human laments did not come out. They began to speak of their unemployed men, without underwear, shoes, anything, of children who tortured them with their disobedience. They wept and clung to us, they wished to show us their homes. It was impossible to decline.

In one of them, Dr. De Luca's assistant, a youth with a cold and irritated demeanor, sloppily dressed, was examining an old man whose end appeared imminent, and who was the uncle of one of the two women, Assuntina. The room was full of people, shadows, who, it seemed, gave off a stench. I couldn't see the dying man, hidden by the crowd and by the doctor, but my attention was drawn to another person; I couldn't call him a man, who, standing behind the doctor, tapped him on the shoulder from time to time. He was a creature of an indefinable age, untidy, strange, with something meek and terrible about him at the same time. His eyes were protected by thick eyeglasses, and one of the lenses seemed twice as thick as the other. He had a fringe of gray hair over his forehead, which got under his glasses, giving his pupils a greater ambiguity. While with one hand he touched the doctor, with the other, the left, he was constantly scratching his chest, with a kind of tic, trying to open his shirt.

Finally the doctor turned.

"You, what do you want?" he said abruptly.

"Bi ... bi ... bi ... bismuth."

"Pass by the clinic later."

"Yes ... yes ... yes ..."

"Speak properly!" a woman said aggressively, coming out from behind a curtain. She was like one of those bitches with countless teats, who drag themselves with solemn sadness from one rejection to the next. Her hair was still golden, but her face was ashen, her eyes spent, her mouth toothless. Her narrow, childlike shoulders were in contrast with the large curve of her belly over the short legs. On her finger, she wore a wedding ring.

"The doc-tor un-der-stands," said the sick man, humbly.

A minute later, the doctor had left, and the shadows had all gone back into their holes, in this case the four corners of the room, which was large, and was divided by means of boxes, old sheets drawn along two poles, and also pages of newspaper, all illuminated by an oil lamp. Assuntina was giving some medicine to her uncle, who smiled stiffly, absorbed, when from right behind that bed, where there was a partition, I heard the sound of anxious, choked, blessed breathing. I stuck my head out a bit, and saw, at the foot of another bed, the syphilitic and his wife. He was sitting on the edge, she was on her knees in front of him, and with her tongue out of her mouth was licking one of his hands. The unhappy man's eyeglasses had fallen off, he was looking up, as if blind, and his whole body trembled.

At the Granili, night was beginning, and the involuntary city was preparing to consume its few goods, in a fever that would last until the following morning, the hour when complaints, surprise, mourning, the moribund horror of living start again.

THE SILENCE OF REASON

EVENING DESCENDS UPON THE HILLS

⌒〜〜⌒

O n the evening of June 19 (evening in a manner of speaking, since the sky was bright and the sun was still high over the sea, its glare intense), I boarded the #3 tram, which runs along the Riviera di Chiaia to Mergellina. I sat in a corner seat next to a woman without a nose, who had an enormous plant in her lap, and I began to think about what I would say to justify my visit to Luigi Compagnone,* who worked in the cultural department of Radio Naples and whom I hadn't

---

* Luigi Compagnone (1915-1998) was a Neapolitan author who was an editor of the magazine *Sud: giornale di cultura*, published from 1945 to 1947.

seen in quite some time, and to whose home, in fact, I was now going. I needed some information about four or five young Neapolitan writers—Prisco, Rea, Incoronato, and La Capria* (whose first novel was just coming out, from a publisher in the north); I didn't exclude Pratolini,† even if the author of *A Tale of Poor Lovers* couldn't call himself Neapolitan, nor was he a writer at the start of his career, but I had learned that he was about to leave Naples permanently, if he hadn't already. For a certain period, Compagnone had entertained all these writers at his home, and I hoped to get from him some particularly juicy bit of news, the

---

* MICHELE PRISCO (1920-2003) was a journalist, film critic, and novelist. His novels described the trials and tribulations of the Neapolitan middle class. In the 1960s, he collaborated with Compagnone, Domenico Rea, and Luigi Incoronato, among others, on the literary review *Le ragioni narrative*.

DOMENICO REA (1921-1994), born in Nocera, was a journalist, novelist, and playwright. He collaborated on various projects with Leo Longanesi, Arnoldo Mondadori, Giorgio Strehler, Italo Calvino, and arranged for writers such as Jack Kerouac, Allen Ginsberg, and Giuseppe Ungaretti to visit Naples and give readings. His collection of short stories, *Gesù, fate luce* (Jesus, Shed Some Light), published in 1950, was a huge success, nominated for and winning many prizes, and was translated into several languages.

LUIGI INCORONATO (1920-1967) was a journalist and novelist who met Compagnone, Prisco, and Rea at the University of Naples. He fought in the Italian resistance during the Second World War and received a bronze medal for bravery.

RAFFAELE LA CAPRIA (1922-   ) was a journalist, novelist, screenwriter, and translator. He wrote for Corriere Della Sera and was one of the editors of the literary journal *Nuovi Argomenti*. He cowrote several screenplays for the director Francesco Rosi.

† VASCO PRATOLINI (1913-1991) was a novelist and screenplay writer who fought in the Italian resistance during the Second World War. His most famous novels were *Cronache di povere amanti* (*A Tale of Poor Lovers*), *Cronaca familiare* (*Family Chronicle/Two Brothers*), and *Le ragazze di San Frediano* (*The Girls of San Frediano*), the latter two of which were made into films. Among the screenplays he worked on were Luchino Visconti's *Rocco and His Brothers* and Roberto Rossellini's *Paisà*. He was nominated for the Nobel Prize in Literature three times.

kind that raises the tone of a piece of writing. "What the Young Writers of Naples Are Up To" was the title of my article, which had been commissioned by an illustrated weekly magazine.

No one could have said that the tram was in a hurry. It was now moving so much more slowly than when I got on at Piazza Vittoria—when its speed had been more or less normal—that one might reasonably suspect the driver had fallen asleep, or was lying wounded in his seat, one eye half open. In reality, the man, in a faded jacket with its buttons missing, was sitting in a normal fashion in the driver's place, but was slowing down more and more because of the poor condition of the roadway, which appeared to be in ruins.

Leaning out the window, I saw, for a stretch of a kilometer or so—about the length of the Riviera di Chiaia—a swarm of half-naked men, with gray backs, gray shorts, gray heads and hands, who were breaking up the pavement. The paving stones were all dislodged, so that the street resembled a raging torrent whose turbulent waters, once rushing obliquely, were suddenly straightened out and petrified. Many streets, when a certain kind of roadwork is done, take on this distressed and destitute appearance. But here something was different, which soon made it necessary to reject those two descriptive adjectives. No, one could speak neither of *distressed* or of *destitute*; this street was, instead, smiling and terrible, much like the expression of intelligence and generosity that the faces of the dead have. It was a *dead* street, or at least that's how I defined it to myself, hoping to be able to find later a less vehement and irrational description, something that turned out to be impossible.

On the right side of the street, I saw the same nineteenth-century houses and late seventeenth- and early eighteenth-century palaces that had gradually replaced the fishermen's hovels that, two centuries earlier, had been so numerous in that area of the city that runs right up against the sea. There was no place more graceful and charming, even after the savage years between 1940 and '45: the hail of tiny holes that marked the façades after the machine-gun bombardments, and the great solemn gaps opened up by the bombs, had for a while animated those walls, harmonizing perfectly with the humans swarming at their base. The thing both dark and brightly colored, that interminable procession of the working class incessantly stirring at the foundations of the buildings, had, for the first time in those years following the tempest of war, emitted a new sound, unexpected and enchanting, like surf rustling on the sand after a hurricane. In that dull, continuous sound was anxiety, but also, even more, hope. That was why the windows of the houses glistened, and the pink and yellow façades were given new vitality when struck by another sun. After several years (it was awhile since I'd been in Naples), the famous Riviera di Chiaia seemed different. A patina, a mysterious concoction of rain, dust, and above all boredom, had spread across the façades, covering their wounds, and returning the landscape to that rarefied immobility, that expressive, ambiguous smile that appears on the faces of the dead. Perhaps if it hadn't been for that eternal Neapolitan crowd that moved on its own, like a snake struck by the sun but not yet dead, amid the distinct presences of a remote age, the landscape would not have appeared so ghostly. But those half-naked men and women and children, those dogs and cats and birds, all those dark, weary, empty forms, all those throats barely emitting a dry sound, all those eyes full of an obsessive light, of an unspoken plea; all those living creatures who dragged themselves along in a continuous motion resembling the actions of someone with a fever, or the nervous mania that possesses certain beings before dying, through a gesture that seems crucial but is never the right one—that great husk of a crowd, those people who cooked, combed their hair, conducted business, made love, slept (though never really slept) in the open air, was always stirring, always disturbing the archaic calm of the landscape, and, mixing human decadence with the immutable decency of things, drew from it that ambiguous smile, that sense of death taking place, of life on a plane different from life, arising from corruption alone.

The sun, shining through a windowpane, momentarily reddened the knees of the woman sitting next to me. She was looking out the window at the street and the silent crowd of workers and poor people who enlivened it. A very slight, self-satisfied smile danced in her black eyes above the scar. With the familiarity common to people for whom *others* exist only for the purposes of conversation—and the conversation is more than anything an endless monologue—she informed me that the roadwork was to be finished by September 8, the day of the Festival of Piedigrotta,* so that the street would be ready for the installation of the special lighting, which this year, thanks to the new mayor, was supposed to be extraordinary. A skinny man sitting in front of us, who looked truly ill, nodded. He whispered the following words, which I quote here more for how strange they sounded on his lips than for their meaning: *"Lassa fa' a Dio"*—Leave it to God. Just afterward, the tram, which had slowed nearly to a stop because of an even thicker crowd of workers, resumed its normal speed. In the meantime the sun had set.

For a few minutes, I was able to see on the left side of the

---

* A popular festival at the S. Maria di Piedigrotta Church. It dates back to the fifteenth century, or even earlier, but its present version began in the 1830s, as a celebration of Neapolitan song. It has since turned into an event that takes place over several days, with concerts, floats, and a songwriting contest.

street dark smudges of trees in the public garden that runs nearly the entire length of the Riviera di Chiaia, separating it from the sea. In the early years of the eighteenth century, this park consisted only of a double row of trees and thirteen fountains placed along the beach by the Duke of Medina. At the end of that century, it was converted into gardens by Ferdinand IV, and since then has been one of the most fabled areas of Naples. On the side nearest Via Caracciolo there is a bridle path still frequented by the aristocracy, while the central paths are continually crowded with the children of the bourgeoisie, riding their bikes and scooters. The children of the working class, from the ages of five to fifteen, happily occupy, instead, the shadiest spots; they go there to pee or to torture animals or to sit around dreaming of love, seduction, and songs. Tuberculosis sufferers are brought there by their relatives on doctors' orders and fade away on the flagstones like white butterfly wings. And although the luxurious building housing the Press Club lends the gardens a dignified air, at night the place is crisscrossed by American soldiers and Neapolitan youths, and is far from safe.

Not even at that moment when the last rays of the sun touched the highest branches of the live oaks, the palms, and the monkey puzzle trees, faintly gilding the decapitated statues and busts, did the place feel safe. And as we approached the far end the gardens became gloomier. Suddenly, I saw this: five youths of an indeterminate age were sitting on a low wall, waiting with totally expressionless faces for the tram to pass. When it neared, one of them stood up and, quickly, imitated by the others, unbuttoned his trousers. Then, taking their cocks in their fingers as if they were flowers, they began to run along the wall, in an attempt to follow the tram, with shrill, sad, passionate cries, wanting to draw our attention to all they possessed.

Not one of the passengers sitting on that side of the tram who saw them mentioned the matter or found it amusing. The driver, who stood up for a moment, fearing that he might have run over someone, sat down with an irritated sigh, and accelerated, so that soon the five troubled souls vanished.

Other boys appeared, with the same pale, rapt faces, and I was afraid of discovering the reasons for their sick intensity. Two of them had hung a small animal from a tree branch and others were intent on skewering a butterfly. Here and there some were urinating. They had no legitimate occupation and were buoyed by a childish madness. Some of them even sang a short hymn to the Virgin Mary.

The noseless woman was observing me quietly, and observing the street, and, observing me and the street together; she must have thought something about what I was thinking, because the smile with which she mentioned the upcoming festival had disappeared, replaced by a fleeting gleam of suspicion. Finally, I realized that she had stopped thinking and was staring me right in the face. Her stare was vacant, and yet her intensity and curiosity made me uncomfortable. The man, too, was now staring me right in the face, then he stared at my hands and feet. I couldn't get upset about it because he looked so deathly ill, but still I found it somewhat annoying. So I didn't wait for the last stop and got off at Piazza Principe di Napoli. The tram continued on without me, and for a moment, as I waited to cross the street, I saw those two blotches—Christian blotches pressed against the window—deep in thought, following me mechanically with their gaze.

Compagnone's apartment was on Viale Elena, the second of the three streets running out of Piazza Principe di Napoli, which are: Via Caracciolo, Viale Regina Elena, and the fork of

Via Mergellina and Via Piedigrotta. While Via Piedigrotta turns toward Piazza Piedigrotta, where the church of the same name is the site of the annual festival, the others flow into Piazza Sannazzaro, near the renowned Mergellina harbor. From this small harbor, originally called Mergoglino, always full of gaily colored boats, and immersed in a silence and light that subdue the colors, the shouts, the splash of oars cleaving the crystal-clear water, the Via Nuova di Posillipo starts, then runs along the entire hill. One could say that here ends working-class Naples (which is all of Naples) and civilized, bourgeois Naples begins, where people do not live in apartment buildings or hovels but only in villas surrounded by large, dark gardens and with their own beachfronts. In actuality, the division is not so precise, since one can find all over Naples beautiful buildings encircled by lush gardens, with marble staircases and drawing rooms, where it's impossible to imagine the gloom and stench of the alleys right outside. Just as in Naples proper the areas of beauty and joy are islands, from Viale Elena onward, the islands, or exceptions, are ugliness and poverty. At Mergellina begin those high walls of yellow tufa, high as the sky, in which are nestled the graves of Leopardi and Virgil, and which protect the gardens of Posillipo from the Phlegrean Fields. These continue on the other side, scattered with spent volcanoes and sulfur springs around the inhabited areas and deserted places alike, in Bagnoli, Pozzuoli, and Cuma.

Compagnone had lived on Viale Elena for several years, but I don't remember if he ever liked it. He lived on the mezzanine floor and was particularly repulsed by the sight of people who appeared while he was sitting at his desk, filthy faces from nearby Mergellina, in stark contrast with the dignity of the neighborhood, and by hearing almost every night shots fired in celebration of one saint or another as the fireworks fell on his terrace. After a while, though, he stopped noticing so much. He was a tall young man, distinguished-looking, with a small head, classical features, and abundant brown hair. His delicately shaped eyes were deep blue and veiled by long lashes. Similarly delicate, and one might even say Greek in form, were his nose and his mouth, whose tightly joined lips only now and again curved slightly at the corners into a murky smile. There was something in his face of both extreme youth and old age, and over the years the struggle between an innate nobility and kindness and an equally strong desperation and malice became increasingly evident, and little by little, especially for those who didn't see him frequently, that baser part of him, like a hidden evil, had advanced. Not by much, however, and one might not even be aware of it.

I crossed Piazza Principe di Napoli to Via Mergellina with the intention of reaching Viale Elena from Via Galiani, which cuts across those two parallel streets and passes right in front of Compagnone's building. I was very near the Caffè Fontana when I thought I saw him. He was coming toward me from the opposite sidewalk, with his usual unhurried, slightly weary, limping gait. His face was pale, as if he was cold, and his eyes looked around joylessly, or rather with a mute, oppressive rage. I was about to greet him when I realized I was simply *remembering* him.

I realized another thing, too: the nonchalance with which I had set out to see Compagnone, as if, as I had believed until then, he was just another Radio Naples bureaucrat—that nonchalance had vanished. I hesitated before turning onto Via Galiani, as if the ground under my feet were moving slightly. Even the buildings seemed to be slightly distorted, and here and there pale, troubled figures looked out, full of resignation and fury.

In that state of mind, between stunned and oppressed, I took a few steps and immediately saw the asphalt at the far end of Viale Elena, and the continuation of Via Galiani, and then, also, the asphalt of Via Caracciolo, illuminated by the blue glow of the sea. The bureaucrat's apartment was situated on that last stretch of Via Galiani, in a building at the corner of Viale Elena. I saw the front gate and the mezzanine terrace. As usual, the gate was ajar, and the terrace was empty. I could have gone in by the main entrance, but I preferred to follow an old habit that, in years past, had led me to enter Compagnone's house only through the gate, where almost every evening and even late into the night it was possible to see the small living room lit up and the bureaucrat sitting in a corner, with a weary, acerbic look, surrounded by his young friends. This time I was not mistaken, the living room was completely dark; not even the smallest ray of light escaped through the door's glass panes, and I could vaguely distinguish only the outlines of the furniture. The doors to the adjoining terrace were also closed, and from the thin lines strung up between the walls not a sock or a handkerchief dangled, leading me to conclude that young Anita, Compagnone's wife, had gone out with the baby. Nevertheless, I pushed open the gate, went up a few steps, pressed the porcelain buzzer set into the wall, and waited, vaguely uneasy, for someone to respond. I didn't feel any vibration, because that doorbell has a special mechanism that allows it to be heard only at the back of the house. Thinking that I might suddenly see the thin figure of the young man emerge, I put my face to the window.

After a few moments, when my eyes had become accustomed to the dark, I could make out the room in all its details.

It was a typical bourgeois living room, full of scrupulously polished old furniture. There were four doors, including the one that led to the street, which looked as if they had been drawn on the pale walls rather than carved into them. The door on the far wall led to a hall and then to the kitchen, where the bureaucrat's family often sat; another door, on the left, separated Compagnone's apartment from the one next door and had been blocked off; the third door, on the right, led to the master bedroom, and no light seeped out of there, either.

Very near the door to the street, the corner of a large table stuck out, covered with a gray wool cloth; on top of it, in a jumble that somehow seemed different from that of the past, were stacks of books, thin sheaves of papers, and the side of a typewriter shut in its case.

On the wall to the right, under a wide dull print of *The Rape of the Sabine Women*, was an old, uncomfortable sofa with its red upholstery fraying in several places. On the opposite wall, facing the sofa, and forming a sort of continuation with the large table, was a white marble console table adorned with a gilt mirror. On the table a bronze clock, decorated with cupids, no longer told the time; the hour hand was broken. On either side of the sofa and the console table were four terracotta medallions depicting the heads of American Indians, life-size, brightly colored, with cold, fixed stares. Actually, everything in that room was cold. Not a rug, a vase of flowers, a lamp, or a painting gave any sign that the owner was happy to live there, or, for that matter, to live: the sensation was of a profound and exalted stillness.

I continued to press my finger on the porcelain doorbell, from which no sound came, and to stare intently and anxiously into that old room.

In the nearest part of the room, precisely around the sofa, I thought I glimpsed some figures, and heard, perhaps, the sound of familiar voices. The singularly slow and chilling laugh, a mixture of a brooding child's and a robot's, belonged to Giovanni Gaedkens.* The young man, dressed in an Allied uniform (bought in the Sanità neighborhood for five hundred lire), was sitting in the middle of the sofa, his laugh a response to a radio sketch written by Luigi Compagnone. Compagnone, with his long legs, still healthy, stretched out in a comfortable position amid the chairs occupied by other friends, was sitting next to Gaedkens. Compagnone sometimes read with a certain malignant grace, sometimes he looked around thoughtfully. On the other side of Gaedkens sat Colonel Prunas's son, as small in stature as a child, unmoving, and strangely mute. At the table was Gaedkens's wife, Lorenza, small, fat, bespectacled, with her hair pulled back; and Anita, Compagnone's wife, a thin, colorless figure, her face meek and cold like a mist-covered hillside. These figures lingered there for a few moments with all the precision and ineffable deceptions of reality; then, like the digits on a taxi meter, they were replaced, without my having seen *how*, by other figures, equally young but not as vivid.

The tall young man with the small birdlike head and a profile that could be either a child's or an old man's is the lawyer Giuseppe Lecaldano, also employed at the radio, a devoted friend of Luigi's and a fervent admirer of Marxist doctrine. The dark, modest-looking man sitting next to him is Alfredo Barra,

---

* GIOVANNI GAEDKENS is actually the poet and writer Gianni Scognamiglio. He is the only one of the *Sud* writers and editors whose name was changed by Ortese in *The Silence of Reason*. Gaedkens was his mother's surname. He was notoriously "mad" and a "genius," and it was rumored that he and Ortese were romantically involved for a brief period.

a skilled laborer and communist, who joyfully witnessed Luigi's first steps into Party life, and, even now that the young man has rejected it, still follows him, as a mourner does a hearse. That cross between the serenity of Phidias and Sartre's depression, those gorgeous lips, those fine eyes, that cold stare, that perfect forehead shadowed by pale bronze curls, that euphoria and that anguish—all belong to the young trade unionist Aldo Cotronei, who once attempted suicide and is newly clinging to the Party for dear life. His melancholy—tender remembrance of a lost beauty, doubt about the grandeur of life—veils those pure features and opens in a sad smile lips accustomed to repeating harsh dogmas. To these people, too, Compagnone would read his radio sketches and then, disgusted, observe them.

The Marxist figures now also dissolved and, with them, the somewhat monotone, rigid voices of people moving in a dream. The room became populated by the most exquisite Neapolitan personalities of the period from 1945 to 1950, among whom could be recognized the city's well-known intellectuals, from Guido Mannaiuolo, the owner of Blu di Prussia, a small modern art gallery, to Gino Capriolo, of Radio Naples; from John Slingher, an Anglo-Neapolitan poet, to Signora Etta Comito, the editor of *Corriere di Napoli*'s literary section; from Samy Fayad, the young Venezuelan, to Franco, Gino, and Antonio Grassi, who were respectively the sons and brother of Ernesto, the dean of Neapolitan journalists. And all these figures also listened to the sketches read by Compagnone, without noticing the disgusted and insulting tone of his almost feminine voice. Then they, too, vanished, and a darkness fell, and in that obscurity the outlines of some near tragic figures were illuminated: the plump, delicate Prisco, with his immaculate manners, the restless La Capria, the pale and boisterous Rea, the communist writers Incoronato and

Pratolini, their expressions cold and callow. Before this group, Compagnone was no longer reading. Seized by an intense but imperceptible tremor, he let the pages full of witty remarks slide from his hands and, overcome by a mysterious terror, he lowered his chin, sharp as an old man's, onto his chest.

THE STORY OF LUIGI THE BUREAUCRAT

I remembered that Compagnone was also a writer, or at least imagined he was, and had only recently decided to dedicate himself to radio sketches. I remembered other things. The reason I had gone there—to obtain information and gossip about young Neapolitan writers—had vanished, making way for a deeper interest that was not without a certain undefined fear. In my mind, it was as if in a vast abandoned house someone had raced by, holding up a lantern. I had to admit that Luigi was not merely a bureaucrat, nor was he entirely a Neapolitan, just as those around him weren't, either, in the same way that the grim route I'd taken a little earlier in the tram revealed more than a Naples of mere color and reck-lessness. Naples wasn't just an onrush of antiquity, it was also the anguished concerns of youth flowing beneath that antiquity.

Compagnone hadn't been a youth like so many, even if like so many he wrote, and had produced the usual poems, articles, stories, and several pages of a novel. Now he wasn't doing much of anything, but there was a time, right after '45, in Naples, when he was very much in the public eye, because everyone had recognized in his agile and audacious prose, in his writing bristling with scorn and anger, the sign of a Naples different from the one that until then had been described in the classics, both ancient and modern, a Naples no longer smiling and enchanted, or drum-beating and grotesque, but as enraged as a whore surprised by the sudden appearance of reason. There was that terrible poem he published in *Sud: A Journal of Culture*, founded and edited by the young Prunas, entitled "This City of Mine is Merciless," expressing something that no one had said since time immemorial about Naples, a city burdened by the myth of ecstatic happiness. There were also stories and articles published here and there that bore the mark of this new consciousness, a glimmer only, but sufficient to kindle hope. At the time, Compagnone was a communist, like for that matter all the tender youths of Naples, formed within the clandestine cells of the Fascist University Group. Once the Germans had left, Luigi hurried directly to that squalid headquarters on Via Galiani to join the Party, with the scrupulousness of a citizen who, having seen his city razed and the enemy artillery finally silenced, approaches the wells, hoping they haven't been contaminated, to begin life anew. His enthusiasm could even at times be annoying, but one couldn't help being touched by it; and as his reputation consolidated and spread—that superior intelligence, that desperate laugh, trembling as if the sky were falling—his apartment soon became a kind of garrison, in close communication with that of young Prunas, stationed in the stronghold of the Nunziatella, the ancient military academy where his father was the headmaster. Surrounding Naples, infamously, was a lava flow of pus and dollars, the Americans having replaced the Bourbons; just hearing a simple "O.K." in English was enough to make all the hearts from Vicaria to Posillipo shudder, and in the homes of these two youths, which in reality were one, they took the opportunity, perhaps naively, but with obvious commitment, to lay the foundations for that school of reason which had already cleansed other towns, and whose absence here was due to the profound lethargy and dissipation of conscience. We wanted to know everything, understand everything about this monstrosity that, in light of recent events, appeared to be Naples; we wanted to remove the finely carved tombstone that lay on its grave and find out if in that rot anything organic remained. For the first time, in the local tradition, words were used such as *sex* instead of *heart, syphilis* instead of *sentiment, obsession* instead of *inspiration*. We discovered that no population on earth was as unhappy as the Neapolitans, and they were unhappy because they were sick; we sought the causes of this sickness, defined the characteristics of this unhappiness, and above all dismantled the myth of happiness and recognized in those existences, and in those songs, an abject despair, the lament of men lost under the spell and indifference of nature, dominated and incessantly drained by a jealous mother. They had become incapable of organizing their thoughts, of controlling their nerves, of taking even a step without stumbling, of participating actively in human history instead of being continually oppressed and humiliated by it. They identified the consequences of this and studied the ways in which mankind could be liberated from such dire enslavement. Right from the beginning, it was clear that culture—understood as knowledge and therefore conscience, a mirror in which to capture one's own image—was utterly indispensable. It was necessary to excise from public opinion the terrible myth of sentimentality, and elucidate all the alterations and distortions that had led Neapolitan society to its present state; and to remove from view, until the general situation improved, the painterly skies of Di Giacomo and Palizzi, proposing instead, and perhaps even imposing, displays of a barren, desperate art. On this, profoundly liberal spirits, such as Compagnone, Prunas, Gaedkens, La Capria, Giglio, Ghirelli,* and others, even if some were devoted to the Marxist faith (let's not forget that in Naples in those years communism was a form of emergency liberalism), agreed with the die-hard militants, who were their intellectual inferiors, incapable of independent thought, and who clung to the idea of a universal state that would replace the reign of the Church over the people. But the militants' anxiousness to recruit new members, along with the enthusiasm and generosity of men who have long endured solitude, led these Party officials to shake the insurgents' hands with silence and a smile which was perceived as a genuinely deep fondness. Each group, from behind its respective barricades, the Party officials in the editorial office of their weekly, *Voce,* and the young rebels in the rooms of *Sud,* in Viale Elena and behind the courtyard of the Nunziatella, seemed for a while to be working toward the same goal, even if their methods and language were at odds.

Prunas, in his little magazine, which had seven issues, each one an adventure, and each one published thanks to the secret sale of some family heirloom, a loan, a promissory note, or a

---

* ANTONIO GHIRELLI (1922-2012) was a journalist who joined the Communist Party in 1942, fought in the resistance, and, after his experiences with *Sud,* eventually moved to Rome and became the editor of *Corriere Dello Sport.* He got his start in journalism in Naples writing for the journal published by the Fascist University Group.

collection taken up among the wealthier of his contributors, had printed, or would print, the first essay in Italy on contemporary English poetry, Sartre's first essay on existentialism, the first pages of Vasco Pratolini's *Family Chronicle*, Compagnone's atrocious *News of Naples*, some of the astonishing modern poetry by the German-Italian Gaedkens. By highlighting this or that name, by digging up or having his colleagues dig up this or that story, trend, or milieu, he was pushing for a return of consciousness, an expansion of literature into the realm of journalism, where, according to him, true life had taken refuge. He wanted to destroy the myths, the superstructures, those gaseous halos which over time collect around a society and distort it. Naples was full of these distortions in the form of ghosts, who occupied the important public offices, keeping the most irresponsible strata of the population terrorized and grieving, and in a state of nebulous, secret corruption.

It is important to note that Prunas was not Neapolitan. From a noble Sardinian family (he would inherit the title of count when his father died), he had developed an enormous fascination with Naples, the pure nature of which was demonstrated by his utter lack of personal or political ambition. At the heart of others' passions (when they even existed), there was always at play the anxiety of a son who, at his mother's deathbed, peers at his siblings and secretly wonders about her will, and then can't help fantasizing about what he may inherit. Prunas, by contrast, with his air of somber passion, racked his brains and was consumed by thoughts of how he could help that great invalid even though he was an outsider. Dressed like a lowly clerk, with never a lira in his pocket (his parents didn't know how to make him get a university degree and return to the fold of decent people), he never missed an occasion to declare his respect for the city, reduced as it was, and to insist that its liberation should not result in some new form of bondage; that cultural independence was essential; that there should be cultural supervision over the government, any government; that culture should control government and not vice versa. All these things he took for granted, perceiving them as obvious, and yet he couldn't stop talking about them. Such ingenuousness (not that his friends didn't agree with him—they certainly did! But they thought he was, generally, getting ahead of himself) began to irritate people and provoke derision. Not only at *Voce* did people start saying that the young man was in the best case another victim of the irresponsibility and frivolousness of an earlier era, that his axioms revealed the weakness of his education; even his own circle of friends, those who formed the editorial staff of *Sud*, began to pull away and, in the silence and ensuing reluctance, to manifest bewilderment, a kind of disillusioned disappointment. Discussions gave way to simple conversations; politics became an excuse for talking about a problem of employment; concerns about one's career or even some minor personal problem became increasingly more important than the problems and future of the journal; and cultural independence, Prunas's anxious credo, and his passionate arguments fell upon ever fewer and less sympathetic ears. The sight of a cheap cigarette still smoldering and reeking under a chair, a cruel reminder of the precariousness of their situation, could set off in their minds a silence profound enough to cause tears, an irrational desire for activity and different thoughts, where the sacrifices of thinking would be generously compensated. Whereas the young Sardinian was able to substitute disheartened passion for material comfort, the Neapolitans could only suffer terribly while formulating a farewell to their youth, which certainly cost them, but was nonetheless essential.

In truth, the high number of returned issues of *Sud* stacked under and around Prunas's bed, in the small dark room to which his parents had relegated him; the shower of contested promissory notes, initially light and autumnal, that was soon a raging deluge of darkest winter; the gossip in *Voce* aimed at him; his family's resentment, exacerbated by the gallant advice from their priest; the letters from a certain baron from Catanzaro, who, "having perused the 'Soviet rag,' expressed his disgust"—all these were, even for the most optimistic soul, unquestionable evidence of failure.

Just as on the beach, at the end of a storm, the sea's high, pounding waves retreat, and only shells, seaweed, and debris remain, and sparkle in the sand, so the most glittering names and personalities distanced themselves from the small rooms of the Nunziatella, leaving in their wake others, who did not shine as they had. Raffaele La Capria, who, for a moment, in his essay *Cristo Sepolto** seemed to express a healthy concern about the bourgeoisie, shut himself up in the grottoes of Palazzo Donn'Anna, where his parents had a very comfortable apartment, and resumed his correspondence with certain Englishmen whom he much admired, while considering fleeing to Rome— which he did some years later—and reinvigorating his violent passion for Proust and Gide, which resulted finally in his first novel, *Un giorno d'impazienza* (*A Day of Impatience*). Giglio and Ghirelli, Marxists with pliable liberal tendencies, returned definitively to the quiet careers they had previously chosen, the

---

* "Cristo Sepolto" (Christ Interred), published in *Sud* in 1945, was inspired by Henry Moore's drawings of refugees in the London underground during the German bombardments of the Second World War.

former to Milan and the latter to Rome. Giovanni Gaedkens, who considered going to Milan but was chained to Naples by poverty (he worked as a substitute teacher), came every day to the Nunziatella to discuss with Prunas abstruse editorial projects. Giovanni, who had a more modest and cordial nature, like the three Grassi brothers and the journalist Mastrostefano, had no trouble finding very good assignments from the local press, and if he and the others still came back to the old editorial office it was only to elicit from Prunas his anguished admiration. Some of the artists remained faithful in their way: Vincenzo Montefusco, a youth who barely owned a pair of shoes and was always solitary and taciturn, and Raffaele Lippi, the son of a *carabiniere*, who in his lodgings in Vasto (the grayest neighborhood in Naples) painted dead cats and ruins.

As for Luigi Compagnone, his reaction was unique.

In the region of the far South where the sun shines brightest, a secret ministry exists for the defense of nature from reason: a maternal genius of limitless power to whose perpetual and jealous care the sleeping populations of the place are entrusted. If this defense were to slacken for only a moment, if the cool, gentle voices of human reason were to get through to nature, it would be destroyed. The miserable conditions of this land are due to the incompatibility of two equally great forces—nature and reason—which are irreconcilable, no matter what the optimists say; and to the terrifying secret defense of the region—ambiguous nature, with its songs, its sorrows, its dumb innocence—and not to the pitilessness of history, which is here mostly "regulated"; these are also the causes of reason's wretched failure whenever it organizes an expedition down here or sends its most ardent pioneers. Here thought is the servant of nature, every book or work of art is a contemplation of it. The smallest hint of a critique, or a slight tendency to correct the heavenly shape of this land—to see the ocean as only water, volcanoes as still other chemical compounds, or man as simply his guts—is killed.

A good part of this nature, of this maternal and conservative genius, takes over the same kind of human and keeps him weighed down by sleep. Night and day she watches over that sleep in order to make sure that he doesn't gain awareness; she is tortured by the laments that the son's trapped consciousness emits from time to time, but she is ready to suffocate the sleeper if he shows signs of movement, or hints at gestures or words that are not precisely those of a sleepwalker. Other causes have been given for the stagnation of these regions, but they have nothing to do with the truth. It's nature that rules over daily life and determines the people's sorrows down here. The economic disaster has no other cause. The proliferation of kings and viceroys, the interminable stockade of priests, the sprouting up of churches as if they were amusement parks, along with the filthy hospitals and the brutal prisons, these things have no other cause. It is here, where the nature of antiquity, the mother of spiritual ecstasy, has taken refuge, that man's reason, in so far as it is a threat to her reign, must die.

Like many of us, Compagnone was born in the Neapolitan alleys, where nature runs riot and man's reason is his sexuality, his conscience, his hunger. Still young, and as handsome and lively as an ancient god, he rebelled against all of it. Fascism, like an ideal incubator, warmed and encouraged his rejection of it and much else. And in the humiliation of the war, he discovered himself to be a Marxist, and therefore a new man, and for a moment, together with his contemporaries, he had wept the sweet tears of one who believes that he has been saved. He seemed to all of us, in his cold enthusiasm, to be a true revolutionary, and we believed that, having conquered Mother Nature, he had safely arrived in the land of reason.

When *Sud* folded, Compagnone's grief was sincere and his emotion palpable, as if someone profoundly dear to him had died. But just as at some funerals, while the procession is moving through the streets, the deceased's most devoted friends are distracted—one straightens the handkerchief in his jacket pocket, another stares at the display in a store window, another chitchats, and still another peers at his watch—so such distractions and idiocies soon appeared in Compagnone's manners and his intelligent face. He continued to host the surviving members of the *Sud* group, first and foremost the pale, silent Sardinian Prunas, and to mourn the journal's premature end, but he couldn't hide an excitement and a joy that, strange as it seems, were directly related to that defeat. In other words, ancient nature, which for a time had tolerated the young man's revolutionary activity, suffering the torments of a mother whose son is rebellious, was now with infinite caution suppressing his exultation and reassuming her dominance. She held up a mirror of excellent workmanship to the Marxist Neapolitan in which the story of the *Sud* group, rather than reflecting the imperceptible and terrifying battle between reason and nature, appeared to portray, as in one of those beloved nineteenth century variety shows, the innocent conflict between the dreams of youth and the overwhelming logic of things. The terms here were reversed. Nature alone was capable of reason, and rebellious thought was placed with the decorative and ephemeral things of beauty on this earth, like pears and apples hanging from eternal branches. As a consequence of his new subjugation to the Neapolitan mystery, Compagnone felt the need to revisit as frequently as possible his and our past, examining all that seemed to him contaminated by that new, dark urge to live, which he deemed folly. Having determined that at the heart of our relationships was the Fascist Student Center on Largo Ferrandina, which had simply been an occasion to bring us together, he found that his goal had been reached, and he recognized in us and in himself the older generation. Going deeper into his analysis, he discovered that we were useless. Our lives appeared to him as if in the caves of Lethe: a swirl of souls, restless ghosts upon nature's deep waters. He perceived Naples and us to be in direct conflict. His relationship to the Party remained, on the surface, intact, but inside that, too, was collapsing. What he liked about the Party was that bit of the chaotic and the colorful that Marxist doctrine had taken from its interaction with our regions, but he was afraid of seeing Marxism wind up under the great dome of a new church, a modern cathedral, where the Neapolitans, worshipping their virtues instead of their vices, would no longer be Neapolitans. In this absurd situation, the former revolutionary, ensconced in the reaction, summoned Party members and rebels alike and began to insult them all, and they lowered their heads and wept. Communists or liberals, we were still Neapolitan communists and liberals, and we loved him too much not to see his insults as the rage and sadness of the sea. Furthermore, we were all weak and maimed. He told each of us our faults, exposed our wounds. That one killed himself, this one was about to, that one stole, this one had been robbed. He was truly like our land, our common mother, the city we had wanted to conquer, and he reminded us of our weaknesses and our shame, so that we would never again dare to rise up against it. He was this, and he was also its son, the son of this land, and as such denied himself forever.

In the literary pages of the local papers, and also in the journal *Il Borghese*,* these cries became increasingly frequent and shrill. No one was spared. He obeyed two exigencies simultaneously: to destroy first our souls and then his own, for having wounded ours. He attacked old and new religions, his own family, and the young writers from *Voce*; he attacked the radio as a government apparatus, and those who were opposed to the radio. He declared a state of madness and general lack of intelligence, but without sympathy, without hope of a resurrection, instead almost taking pleasure in all that resembled silence, monotony, death, the end of reason.

He was consumed by this passion. He honed it, and, by dint of long and diligent study, tried to make it more beautiful and attractive. Voltaire and Flaubert became his idols, and he sought in them new ways of bringing his compulsion to offend to the level of an art. But it happened that the city, those places both old and new that he had wanted to tear apart, became accustomed to this phenomenon, and the enemies he had hoped for disappeared. Instead, people became bored, and this distressed him more than the earlier tears and anger. In the indulgent and affectionate smiles of people he had intended to torture, he saw the ability to get used to anything, the ancient impassivity toward insult and pain, which forms the essence of Naples, and so he saw the uselessness of insults or wounds. He felt the same terror as one who has flung himself at a puppet swinging from a tree and suddenly discovers that it is not a puppet but the corpse of a hanged man, and he feels something around his own neck and realizes that he himself is hanging from the branch of a tree. He continued to laugh, but his laughter rang false.

---

* The Bourgeois

Around the same time, while playing soccer in the courtyard of his building with some friends, Luigi hurt one of his knees. It didn't seem to be anything serious, but a few months later they were talking about synovitis. The leg was put in a cast. When the cast came off, the leg was slightly shorter than the other one, enough to throw his youthful figure off balance and to cause him profound anxiety. He also began to experience early signs of arthritis, which soon spread to his hands, slightly altering their shape. He continually looked at them and could think of little else. Even with his friends, both the political and the literary types, he could speak only of his ailments and despised any-one interested in things other than health and physical training. He regained a kind of superficial interest in the Communist Party, raising many hopes throughout the federation, but it passed as quickly as it came. During this period, in which he seemed to have totally lost his elegant sense of proportion and control, he threw himself into passionate readings of the New Testament, and his Marxist or liberal friends who came to visit him in the evening would find him wrapped in an enormous woman's shawl, his demeanor feverish, his eyes those of a febrile and rapt child, and they would be forced to listen to this or that passage from the Sermon on the Mount and I don't know how many sayings of St. Paul's. He clung to those ancient texts, hoping to find in them salvation. He was possessed by a vague preoccupation with the brevity of human life and its precipi-tous pace toward the end, which is the foundation of Naples' obstinacy, and gives it that callousness, that kind of dead fury, and in the Gospels he sought a way to forget about his hands. Once the arthritis had stabilized, however, the immediate terror and thoughts diminished, and the sacred texts went back up on a shelf. Not that he was cured, but whether it was the arrival of spring, which appeared on the sea, making it tense and brilliant, lengthening the days and causing the nights to be sweeter, or the shame of those tremors, which had made him a boy again, and which he now acknowledged were exaggerated, the young man suddenly changed. Kicking aside the chair on which he rested his injured leg, he began, with the help of a cane, to resume his visits to the radio, on Corso Umberto I, at the other end of Naples. That slight difference between one leg and the other, changing his stride and making it more difficult to walk, caused his face to twitch, which he tried to hide, and to assume that sad, careless expression that he never lost thereafter. Youth and its passions were gone. He now saw himself as a *worker* and viciously sought confirmation of this truth from every Italian, and particularly from every Neapolitan. The beautiful Marxists of the past, Lecaldano, Cotronei, and Barra, who, with the fervor of neophytes, still visited his dark apartment, hoping to win over his spirit, annoyed him and the liberals as well, and he listened to them distractedly for hours, staring at his hands or twisting a finger until it cracked. He didn't enjoy anything anymore, had no expectations, and it was likely that nothing new would have happened for years in his disconcerting existence if, precisely during his convalescence, the star of Domenico Rea hadn't risen rapidly, like a fireball across the night sky of Naples. Rea's book *Gesú, fate luce* (*Jesus, Shed Light*), with a preface by the critic Francesco Flora, was published, and no one in Naples could talk about anything else.

That part of Luigi which no longer found anything to hold on to, having ripped up everything around him, and was therefore dying, was gripped by the fury and force of the pages of the author from Nocera, by their vivid and raw resurrection of the Neapolitan myth. At the same time, a deep silence, an anguish without form or voice, lodged in his mind. It wasn't envy but a contempt that he was no longer able to express, a furious yet paralyzed melancholy. He *had* to like Rea, *had* to honor Rea, *had* to acknowledge Rea as the most legitimate voice in Naples. This, then, was the result of the years of a bitter and victorious fight against what he'd labeled the *nullity*, the Neapolitan middle class: the barefoot youth of *Sud*, the poor souls of *Voce*, many clerks, students, the restless crowd in Naples that was no longer truly Naples, and hated Naples; was no longer colorful but full of anguish and trivial thinking. The populism and naturalism that he had wished for were unexpectedly served up by Rea on a fourteenth century platter, and it was impossible for him to reject them. As had happened under Fascism, his desperate intelligence and real critical ability, roused by that irruption of antiquity, wanted to intervene, to take a stand, to oppose, but they were no longer at his command. He had to accept Rea, noting that it was useless to do otherwise, and he persisted in the game that shifted the rules, conceding all authority to the false, and stripping the truth of every right. And so it was that we witnessed this fragile revolutionary, who contained within himself both nature and a hatred of nature, by which I mean instinct and a critical ability, lavish a fiercely enthusiastic admiration on this populist Rea, whom he welcomed to his house and imposed on all his friends, spending many days with him, his wife, and his motor scooter. And when his friends, seeing his discomfort, said to him: "Come on, Luigi, Rea isn't so great," he would raise his cane and threaten them. He fell ill again, because of this, and became scrawny and weak. As for the author from Nocera, healthy as an ox, and very content with how his life was unfolding, he pitied Luigi, because he had a kind heart, but he also despised him, and if he spent time with him it was because he sensed in Luigi that critical faculty whose approval was infinitely important to him. But the man who welcomed him into his home was not the ancient god of whom he had heard so much and who now praised him; he was just another Neapolitan like him. And because of this, the conversations and interviews between the two of them were never real or honest, leaving Rea irked and dissatisfied and Luigi ever more neurotic and full of dark thoughts.

This was the memory I had of Luigi, and now, as an outsider, after being part of his life for so long, and having finally forgotten him, I found myself again at his door.

CHIAIA: DEAD AND RESTLESS

I took my finger off the doorbell and my hand off the wall, marveling at the fact that I had been there so long (a lot of time must have passed, because the sky had turned green), and anxious to go down the steps as quickly as possible, return along Via Galiani, and take the first tram I could back to the city center. I was thinking that I could put off my visit until the following day, but in the most secret part of my soul I had determined never to set foot in that place again.

Thought and action, however, were stillborn. In a kind of inner silence, made up of aversion and concentration, I had to acknowledge that the apartment was no longer deserted. In the halflight of that room, there was now a young man in shirtsleeves, his thin face bowed, who was looking at the door in bewilderment. Maybe he had been there for a while and I hadn't noticed. I hadn't seen him, and he had recognized and observed me, even if not a line on his face, nothing, absolutely nothing, indicated the least interest or pleasure. I remembered that we had fought once, but that did not justify such a deadly cold-ness—the coldness of those who, rather than flee the world, watch it shrink and fade, and, turned to stone, do not dare to raise even a lament.

After a moment, a smile crossed that face, which was more detached and dead than that of any in Chiaia, and I saw that the young man was coming to the door, limping. He was holding a cigarette, and he flicked it away as he opened the door.

"Please, come in," he said, continuing to smile in *that way*, his gaze everywhere but on me, as he held out a sweaty hand. "Sorry, my hand is sweaty. How are you?"

"Me? I'm fine." Entering, I felt around me a horrifying atmo-sphere of cellars and graveyards. "Very well," I said, rather upset.

"Anita must be in the back with the kid."

"That's what I thought when I saw you come in," I said, not making much sense. "And you? How are you?"

I sat down near the large table, and I thought I shouldn't look at him, so I turned my back. I couldn't see him but I felt him, though more like an absence than a presence. It was as if behind my back there were an abyss, a chasm full of hands clapping, which created a desolate sound, an endless sigh. To give myself courage, I looked at the things around me, but they merely reconfirmed that subtle feeling of death, that indeter-minate point in life when the unknown dimension, the silence of death, arrives. Only the gaze of those four Indians hanging on the wall was alive at that moment—but even they seemed distraught.

Since he hadn't responded to my question, and I could hear him pacing, I thought it would be best to minimize my thoughts and my energy, to banish from my mind, or at least relegate to a tiny corner, any words related to the living world, which could only upset him. I would calm him by showing him that, owing to life's exigencies, I, too, had been intellectually humiliated and conquered. I would have to appear cold, without strength or joy.

"Luigi," I said, looking at the ambiguous forms of the gray print of the sofa reflected in the mirror, "I need to ask you for some information that only you can give me. That's why I've come."

"Ah, yes?" he said. "What information? I'd be glad to help. Something to do with the radio, I imagine?"

"No, nothing to do with the radio."

He walked in front of me and went to sit in a corner of the sofa.

"So what is it then?"

Without looking at him (I could just see him in the mirror in front of me), I told him that I was planning to write something about the Neapolitan writers whom he also knew, and whose names had emerged from the hills of Naples and were heard with pleasure in Milan and Rome. In the mirror, I saw his thin, sweating face quiver and his eyes open greedily, like someone who sees something glitter in front of him. But his voice, when he spoke, was completely indifferent and calm.

"Prisco and Rea, of course."

"And also Incoronato and La Capria."

"I see."

"I don't think there's anyone else."

"No, I don't think so."

"It's for an illustrated weekly," I thought I should explain.

"The public adores hearing about these people. We may think it's fatuous, but we have to consider what the public wants."

"Yes, I agree," he said.

The mirror seemed to have dimmed. In its surface the young Radio Naples bureaucrat now appeared slightly paler, even more hunched, and indescribably exhausted. I stopped staring at the mirror, and cautiously turned to look at him. Although it seemed impossible, in just a few minutes something had drastically changed in him. The statue who had opened the door to me was now alive and trembling. It was as if he were seeing something of enormous magnitude right in front of him. His blue eyes were lowered, and his refined face emanated an exceptional alertness. That thin, polished, beautiful face, prematurely aged by malice and boredom, was now awake and thoughtful. That seated body, slightly off balance and twisted by ill health, seemed to be losing, moment by moment, its weakness and impassivity, as if it were about to hurl itself at something. He exhibited a kind of sleepy despair. I stared at him attentively, ready for a gesture or word that, coming out of that misery, might surprise me. And so I asked him:

"Are you not writing anymore?"

"For now, no," he said quickly, as if just waking.

He got up and went to the front door, where he stood for a moment looking through the window at Via Galiani, then he came back. I regretted my question, and looked at him in confusion.

"You need information ... I mean precise information ... facts for your article," he said graciously.

"Yes," I mumbled, "information ... facts."

His expression was kind, generous.

"Well, you are mistaken," he said smiling. "I don't have any."

He sat down again, at the far end of the sofa, and crossed his legs. He was behaving just like a child who sees a tiger in his room, or a huge spider on his rocking horse, but, for some deep reason (an even greater terror, perhaps), he *can't* reveal that he has seen the object of his fear. First of all, he continuously avoided looking at me, and then he was upset and then anxious. It was as if, seeing in me something hostile, he were hearing the sound of bells coming up from the floor. And yet complete silence reigned in the room.

"Luigi," I said, a few minutes later, looking at the notebook he had on his lap, looking at it very attentively, even if it was just an old notebook, "might you at least give me some information about your life? I confess that I've forgotten most of it. And yet it's important. I'd like to write about you, too, in this article."

"Ah!" he said.

Then added:

"Why?"

And when I didn't respond:

"Whatever for?"

Just then the door opened and in came the radio bureaucrat's young wife, dressed in yellow. She didn't seem at all surprised to see me. Perhaps she had heard me from the kitchen and hadn't come right away because she was busy cleaning up or feeding the child. In her yellow dress, her face smooth and even, like a face in a modern painting, she had about her a look of calm that revealed neither mirth nor thought. Her hair was so thin you could see her scalp, but this softened her high forehead. She had come in to say something to Luigi, but seeing me she forgot what it was, and, quickly drying her wet hands on her apron, she came toward me. "How well you look," she began, "it's been forever since I've seen you around here, but just yesterday I was thinking of you." She stared at me with her extremely tranquil, pale eyes. At her appearance, Luigi had huddled in a corner of the room and stopped talking while painfully cracking first one hand and then the other.

"Perhaps I've interrupted you," the young woman said, noticing our strange silence. She looked at us slowly while reflecting. "Luigi, don't do that with your hands," she added after a moment, "you know I can't stand those affectations."

"Sorry," the bureaucrat said swiftly, and let his hands fall. Then he raised them again and stared at them in his usual obsessive way. "Sorry."

"I interrupted you while you were talking ... Was it something important?" his wife repeated quietly.

"Absolutely," responded Luigi, "absolutely. She," and he pointed at me, "has to write an article on the intellectuals of Naples and has come to ask me for suggestions ... information."

"Do you have anything to tell her?" his wife asked with interest.

"Of course I do ... of course I can tell her things," the bureaucrat responded, smiling.

She stopped paying attention to him.

"And will you write about Luigi?" she said, turning to me, with a stare that was more transparent but cold. She was mentally calculating what I could do for him. In her low voice there was an imperceptible quiver, a question. "He doesn't know how to promote himself," she continued, somewhat agitated. "He cares nothing for money, as if he didn't have a family. And he writes no worse than others. You weren't here, but the other night he began reading to us the first chapter of a novel he began in '44 ... Lecaldano ... Barra ... they were here. They found it entertaining. He could finish it now."

From the kitchen, we heard the child cry out: "Mamma! Mamma!"

"I'm coming ... Tell him to finish it, won't you?" the young woman urged me, as she left.

When the two of us were alone again, I saw that Luigi had lowered his head.

He didn't seem to remember his desperate "Why? ... Whatever for?" which for a moment had brought him back to life. Something had shattered inside him, the anxiety of a moment before had fractured, and silence had returned to dominate his memory. Even my presence had ceased to disturb him; he had become perfectly indifferent. Suddenly he stood up and, walking like a weary bird, made his way to the old table, rummaged through some papers for a moment, then took out a page on which he must have written something. His hand, like an old man's, was trembling almost imperceptibly, and, clutching the paper, he asked if I had a notebook and pencil.

"These are notes about Rea ... I wrote them down for my own use. Unfortunately, only about Rea. But you'll agree that Rea is very important—in fact, besides him other writers really don't exist in Naples."

I didn't respond right away, but then, seeing that he was waiting, I said, "Oh, yes, certainly."

He stared anxiously at me for a moment, then began pacing up and down the room, with his frantic, unsteady gait, while he dictated. He dictated in a voice that was incredibly cold, mechanical, monotonous, yet transparently still full of hate and pain, as if every word were hammering home an ancient death sentence that hung over him. And as he dictated he would sometimes look at the paper, sometimes cast profoundly sad and troubled glances at the ceiling. Here is what I find written in my notebook:

"Notes on the writer Domenico Rea.

"Rea was born in Nocera Inferiore on September 8, 1921. He has already written three books: *Spaccanapoli*, *Le Formicole rosse*, and *Gesù, fate luce*. In the autumn another book of his will be published, which was commissioned by Fabbri, a publishing house in Milan. This publisher specializes in pedagogical works and textbooks. Fabbri himself, the head of the publishing house, asked for a pedagogical type of book from Rea, because he had been particularly impressed by some stories of Rea's that were set in the world of childhood. This is how Rea came to write *Anticuore*. The publisher, De Amicis, suggested this title, and Rea now has infinite respect for him.

"However, if Rea had had to choose a title, it would have been called *I 51*, because it tells the story of the fifty-one boys who went to elementary school with him."

"To elementary school," he repeated.

His words continued on, fading little by little into a kind of murmur, in part because the tension was broken, in part because of the voices and figures that had for several minutes been animating the street outside and were vaguely visible in the dim square of the window.

"Look ... look," I heard him say all of a sudden, thoughtfully. He had lowered the hand that was clutching the piece of paper and moved with curiosity to the window. I stood up and joined him.

Coming down Via Galiani was a group of kids, barefoot

and bold, from the nearby neighborhood on the sea. At the front was a girl of about seven, her head closely cropped, and wearing a gray rag that, leaving her chest bare, came down to her feet in the manner of a queen. Evidently the leader of the band, she carried a stick at the top of which was a very small image of St. Anthony, all gilded, but now dulled. Since it was still the week in which the saint was celebrated, she and her companions were asking passersby for donations in his name. As they walked, and begged, they let out cries of laughter, their pleas at once clownish and desolate, as they paraphrased in dialect one of the many Christian hymns to the Virgin:

Heavenly Virgin
have pity on us ...

and they emphasized the word *pity* by doubling over with laughter every time they said it.

"Look ... look!" Luigi repeated.

And then added: "Truly entertaining."

And a little later: "So colorful, so perfect."

While he was saying this, the girl, like a capricious sideshow freak, swiftly left the group and, with a dirty hand outstretched, feigned begging, her toothless mouth open in a soundless laugh. Having glimpsed Luigi, she came skipping up the steps to the window and, holding up her skirt, curtsied. Then she spat.

Luigi watched as her saliva rolled down the window. Together we listened to the sound of those bare feet on the pavement and the childish laughter, both depraved and sweet, as they grew distant.

Anita came back into the room.

"I was thinking," she said, moving toward us, "that we could all go over to Rea's place this evening. Annamaria"—Rea's wife—"has been begging me to call her. It's the perfect occasion."

She broke off, as she had before, in the face of our silence.

"You can't see a thing in here," she said, and in fact it was very dark. She turned on the light and the first thing her eye landed upon, who knows why, was the spit on the window.

"They were spitting," Luigi said. "Some kids ... "

And he sat down again at the far end of the sofa.

There was silence. Anita never wasted time on useless matters. And so, turning to Luigi, she said, "Aren't you coming?"

"No, I'm tired."

"Then I'll go to my mother's."

"That would be best," the bureaucrat said courteously.

She appeared perplexed.

"And what's this?" she asked, bending down to pick up off the floor the piece of paper with the notes about Rea, which had somehow fallen to the ground.

"I don't know. Maybe it's a message from the milkman."

We heard the child yelling again: "Mamma! Mamma!"

"O.K., goodbye," she said, letting the piece of paper drop. "See you again soon," she said to me.

As soon as Anita left, Luigi asked, "Would you look at my head?" His voice was a combination of infinite patience and infinite terror, as he struggled to achieve a calm that was completely unnatural. "Is there something ... something wet?"

"There's nothing. I assure you."

"It seemed to me ... I felt ... " he stammered. "Now go away, go away."

As soon as I was out of the house, I began to run.

My tears were held back by something stronger than the desire to cry; an imprecise fear of that sweet air, that clear sky, those long hills like endless waves that contained within their serenity so much anxiety and horror. And yet everything seemed so gay and harmonious. Not only Via Galiani but, suddenly, even the interminable Riviera di Chiaia had changed. Where before I had seen only uniformity and petrified desolation, now everything was chaos and dark fascination. I didn't take the tram but set off on foot and, to tell the truth, I no longer knew where I was, if I was coming or going, if it was dawn or dusk, if it was the time of the American invasion or a pristine Greek evening. Or if, rather than Neapolis, I was in Barcelona or Tunis, amid a tiny clamorous crowd of Arabs. It was the hour when Naples lights up and swells like a jellyfish, and the city's wounds shine, and its rags are covered with flowers, and the people reel. In the streets there was a sensation of movement and excitement, which on closer examination was nothing. The crowd of workers and out-casts overflowed from the alleys and, on the more elegant streets, mingled with the bourgeoisie and the aristocrats, who displayed no irritation or disgust, because they didn't even notice them. Many simply remained on the thresholds of those alleys, which are the veins of Naples; some fanned themselves with a piece of cardboard, others slept on the sidewalks with their mouths open, some ate, some sang sad lullabies. In the rooms, next to the beds, some were cooking, and some, at times even young men, lay on the beds thinking. The part of the population that, instead, was going toward the city center in an inexhaustible search for pure air and sweeping views didn't speak or shout in the manner often attributed to Neapolitans. Silent and tired, they walked beside the walls, their faces contorted and pale, lit up by black-circled eyes that were too big, as in a cartoon, their bodies unwashed, their clothes faded by use and stiffened by dirt. You would not have said that they were awake, but rather that they were moving about restlessly in a bad dream.

Who, then, or what, was creating that vague continuous sound that churned the air like the wind when it whips up the sea? It was the radios, the barrel organs, the street-corner violins, the carriage wheels on the cobblestones, the car horns, the useless howls of a dog hit by a shower of stones thrown by a boy. It was a boy rolling in the dirt, his mother telling her neighbor a dream, two girls talking about a man. The city suddenly drowned itself in noise, in order to stop thinking, like a despondent man getting drunk. But that noise dense with chatter, calls, laughter, or simply mechanical sounds was not happy or serene or good. A horrible silence lay beneath it, a paralyzed memory, and a frenzy of hope. It couldn't last long and in fact it slowly faded away.

Night had fallen by the time I returned along Via Filangieri and found myself on the celebrated Via dei Mille, a street that, I believe, owes its name to the fact that Garibaldi's Thousand passed along it on a September morning in 1860. But no more noises, no more sounds, for a long time now, on this monumental, cold street. Only the methodical footsteps of some of the city's notables now deprived of every function except the decorative. Caffè Moccia, one of the street's greatest attractions, cast a gentle blue light across the sidewalk. The place, shaped like a horseshoe with the curved side facing the street, was deserted except on one side of the horseshoe, which had wrought-iron tables painted red. Two people were standing there engaged in friendly conversation. Looking through the front window more closely, I recognized John Slingher, whom in my memory I had caught a glimpse of once at the Via Galiani apartment. Now I saw him in flesh and blood, even if he was a man dedicated to dreams, impeccably dressed (wearing a gray suit and a pearl-colored tie), slowly sipping coffee. In front of him stood Gino Capriolo, a middle-aged man with a robust and melancholy appearance, who was famous for his humor program, *Only in Naples*, written in dialect. It aired every Sunday at lunchtime on Radio Naples, accompanied by a large number of "Letters from Listeners," pleading for help for this or that charity case. There were cancer patients asking for medicine, the unemployed asking for mattresses for their beds, aging down-and-out thugs timidly asking for a couple of pounds of pasta for their tubercular grandchildren or for an old song to be played that reminded them of their youth, and so on. The Neapolitans called this program "human interest," with the same satisfaction the corrupt use when pronouncing pure and elevated words. In the relative silence on the street and in the café, it wasn't difficult for me to gather the gist of the conversation between these two old intellectuals. They were discussing a rather subtle question: how the Neapolitan dialect could become, if elaborated, a language. They cited Di Giacomo and Rea.

The two men moved away and, sitting behind them at an empty table, I spied the young Vincenzo Montefusco, who once numbered among the *Sud* contributors. Tall and ugly as a bird, spectacles perched atop a large nose as if they had been formed as one, he had the strange, intense expression of a man who believes he is alone. He continually turned or raised his head as if someone were calling him, a tic he had had since his father, an honorable civil servant, was shot by the Germans. But no one was ever there. I remembered his bad paintings, the red of his nudes which made them look like damned souls, but instead they were women, women from Naples; and his *Crucifixion*, with the shadow of the three crosses transformed into gallows from which hang three modern Neapolitans. Of course, he wasn't drinking coffee because he didn't have the money, and Cardillo, the waiter, let him be.

Cardillo, a little man with a worn, pathetic face that was perhaps a bit paler than necessary, stood in a corner. And, leaning against a wall with a napkin over his arm, he looked in turn at each of the two old men, and at the young man with the long neck whose head occasionally snapped up and around. I couldn't say that a thought passed through his eyes, but certainly planted on his lips was a faint smile, unconsciously astonished and compassionate, like someone who from on high sees dead cities on vast open plains, glimpses the remains of necropolises, fallen statues, circling crows. Perhaps none of that was true, and he was thinking of his former life, of his kids, but nevertheless he *appeared* so to me. And in my doubt that he was thinking and seeing what I saw, I stared at him in fascination. The two men then stopped talking and started to walk toward the door. This fact pulled me out of my reverie, and, agitated by the idea of being recognized and greeted by them, I left the window and continued on my way.

But I didn't want to keep walking (I felt rather tired) as far as Piazza Amedeo, surrounded by buildings on three sides, the fourth a looming hillside with cliffs, strange vegetation, and flowers. There, with absolutely bourgeois decorum, Naples ended. I turned back down Via Filangieri, and since by now the few lights had been turned on, I could see clearly, in the doorway of one of the buildings, Guido Mannaiuolo, the owner of Blu di Prussia, the small modern art gallery that I mentioned early in these pages. A tall, handsome man who somehow reminded me of an English sea captain of the seventeenth century, with his blue eyes, at once affectionate and cold, he was holding in his white hand a black fan, riddled with holes, and with it he fanned himself now and again, never missing, as he sat idly and mused, the outfits and hairstyles of the ladies who passed before him on the sidewalk. Perhaps he was waiting for someone who had not yet showed up; or he had come out into the doorway simply to get some fresh air (his boutique was in the building's inner courtyard). The day had been very hot, and I seemed to discern on that ivory skin, on those straight thin lips, in that slightly heavier figure, some signs of an exhaustion and perspiration that were not due to summer alone.

"My dear," he said with extreme kindness when I was close by, "I saw something superb just a little while ago, an exquisite black shawl with red sprigs of nettle and a single rose near the fringe. It was like a night without hope protected by bright memories. I'm sure you would love it. Buy it, oh, do buy it!"

He suddenly remembered that some time had passed since he had last seen me, and some kind of process of identification took place in him.

"But you've changed," he said, somewhat disturbed. "I almost didn't recognize you. Isn't it true, Paolo?" he said, slowly turning toward someone hidden in the shadow of the doorway. And looking where he was looking, I saw Paolo Ricci, one of the most notable painters of communist Naples, a tall, red-haired man with a sensitive look about him, who at one point could always be found in *Voce*'s editorial offices but who had disappeared some time ago, and was living quietly in his rooms in the beautiful Villa Lucia.

I don't know why, but I seemed to detect on that face a secret fury, the suspicion that he was pitied, and the pain of having to spend his time with the good Guido, because in Naples conversation was no longer possible. He looked at me and said nothing; rather, he turned his face toward the wall.

"But good, very good, I'm pleased," Guido, smiling his sweet smiles, went on in his dreamy tone, in the terribly distracted manner of one who suffers but no longer understands why. "You'll stay for a while, I hope. How do you find Naples? And Luigi, have you seen him?"

"I saw him," I said.

"He's well, I imagine?"

And when I didn't respond, he said, "He seems much lighter in spirit."

And he continued to stare at me with a look that was even sweeter than the rose he had mentioned earlier, but at the same time perfectly sad, even dead: "His wit, his style, his serenity ... *C'est vraiment éclatant. C'est Naples même.*"—"It's really exciting. It's Naples itself."

He closed the fan and very thoughtfully, full of an anguish he couldn't hide, went back into his boutique.

WORKER'S IDENTIFICATION
CARD NO. 200774

∽⌣⌣∼

The next day was overcast, yet full of dazzling reflections from a confused and troubled light. The sharp sad cries of street vendors rose from all directions. The light that filtered through the immovable clouds was so intense that I had to lower my eyes to go forward. In that painful splendor, the buildings on Via Roma, once Via Toledo, where I got the #115 bus to Rea's house, on Via Arenella, seemed like a mountain of tufa about to collapse. The ten thousand balconies and windows shimmered, as did the shop windows, the café and restaurant signs, and newspaper stands. But it was a lonely shimmer, as if in an abandoned city. It was strange but in many ways the people I saw didn't seem human. I saw them walking slowly, talking slowly, saying goodbye to one another ten times before they actually parted, and then they started talking to one another again. Something seemed to have been broken or never to have been at all: a secret motor that substitutes action for speaking, thinking for imagination, self-doubt for smiling, and restrains color so that everything becomes a line. But I saw no line; I saw a color whirling so fast that it became a white or black point. The greens and reds, because of the rapidity of the whirling, had become rotten; the blues and yellows appeared exhausted. Only the sky, at times, was alive, the light from it such that I had to shield my eyes.

The bus took me to Piazza Medaglie d'Oro, and from there, in order to get to Via Arenella, I had to retrace my steps. Very near the Vomero, the most modern neighborhood in Naples, was dark and enduring countryside; vegetable patches, a few low houses, walled gardens, the yellow and red of carnations sprouting here and there, of women's garments. The eyes of the women and girls were full of furious life without the least bit of harmony. From a balcony, a woman called out to a younger woman dressed in yellow and red who was hanging out laundry in the garden. She responded, almost singing, "I'll be right up." After a moment, from the balcony, the woman shouted back unexpectedly and in dialect: "Here's hoping you spit blood." I looked at the woman who had tossed off this omen and she was calm and collected.

Rea's house was at the far end of a string of vegetable patches, in a recently constructed building marked with the number 77. He had bought it not long before, with some prize money, and spoke enthusiastically about it. Looking up, I saw a row of white balconies with clotheslines strung between them, as I'd seen at

Luigi's, and hanging from them were socks and underwear. A drop of water, which was not rain, fell on my hand. It was noon and not a shout, a voice, could be heard. More drops fell. It was the laundry.

I had the feeling that the family was having lunch and that my visit would be awkward. I even wondered if I should come back later. I looked up again at the socks, and at the tainted light that spread through the dwarf trees, at those gardens, and at the landscape that was simultaneously sensual and gloomy. I went in.

The door I knocked at was on the top floor. I waited not even a second before it opened suddenly, with a nervous jolt, and right away I saw Rea's wife, Annamaria, who was identical to Cora in his story "A Neapolitan Scene": "beautiful, thin, small, covered in pale and silky flesh." Her large black eyes had in them a sliver of white light, a veil almost, as if the young woman were lonely, or had been traveling for a long time and, exhausted, was desirous of quiet and sleep. Even before speaking to me, she turned back and it was then that I saw Rea.

The young man was leaning against the wall in the small hallway staring at me. I had never seen anything with a nature so real, precise, immobile, immutable, and cold, except perhaps a nail. He had one of those terrible, small faces—pale, slightly contorted, and pockmarked, a condition far worse among the working classes. Behind his glasses, his piercing dark eyes appeared to be all pupil. What struck me most was their strange expression, somewhere between the extreme seriousness of animals and a human anxiety and circumspection. He was well-dressed in new clothes: striped gray-blue trousers, an ivory-white shirt, a light-brown wool vest, and pale suede shoes.

"You're here," he said, with the same coldness as Compagnone, concealing his alarm. And he continued to stare at me without smiling.

All of this lasted no longer than a lightning flash, and if I'd been paying less attention I might not have noticed it. He pulled himself away from the wall and, *smiling*, came to greet me. His wife, whom I prefer to call Cora rather than Annamaria, also smiled, and invited me in.

"You must forgive me," I said, embarrassed, "for coming at lunchtime. But you don't have a telephone and I wasn't sure what to do. Luigi sends you his best." I said the first thing that came to mind, in order to dissipate my embarrassment, and to my surprise Rea didn't seem to notice the mention of Luigi's name.

"Come in, come in. We're just having lunch. Pratolini is here, too."

I was led into a tiny, whitewashed kitchen, typical of low-income housing. The Tuscan writer, in his shirtsleeves, was sitting at the head of a small table placed against a wall, with a vague, melancholic smile on his face amid a cloud of steam rising from a large tureen full of pasta. Cora placed a bottle of red wine on the table and a plate of yellow pears, which considerably brightened the setting. Pratolini's jacket was hanging on a nail behind him, and I could read the headlines of the communist newspaper *L'Unità*, which was sticking out of a pocket. Farther behind him, the glass panes of a French door reflected part of a terrace between two white walls under a muggy sky. I looked around, smiling, not because I was at ease but because I still felt Rea staring at me with a strange anxiety, perhaps an effect of the glint of his spectacles, behind which were those hard, piercing eyes that had observed me in the hallway. Like all those who come from nothing to sudden fame and fortune, Rea was never serene and continually asked others for reassurance, which they sometimes couldn't offer, or, if it was forced, seemed tentative. In that tentativeness he saw ill will, and he would furiously defend himself, ending up less certain and more unhappy than ever. The sight of me must have provoked in him a whole new wave of stress. Still watching me, he sat down and began to break up a piece of bread with his small hands, apparently distracted yet quietly alert.

While Cora pulled another chair up to the table and added a plate for me, I turned to Pratolini, whose slightly melancholic smile made me think that he wasn't feeling entirely at ease that morning, either, and I asked him a few questions to which he responded that what I had heard about a move to Rome was indeed correct, that he had left Naples for a place on the Via Appia. He'd finished the much anticipated novel about Naples, but—and here I thought a certain adolescent shame darkened his brow—he felt that so many years of living on Piazzetta Mondragone hadn't ultimately revealed the city to him, and he believed now that his work would always remain that of a desolate and remote outsider. It was an enormous city, the largest and most impressive in the world, because of its pagan seed, and was Christian only in the marks of its wounds; and, strangely, he still couldn't understand what sort of tree had grown from that seed, nor could he say to what species its smooth leaves, its soft fruit belonged. He stopped at this image, and while I wholeheartedly approved of it, I noticed that Rea, elbows on the table, was staring at me, intent on a single thought, and in his stare was that look of anxious suffering that I recognized, to seize someone else's judgment of him, whatever it might be, in order to strangle it at birth, even if afterward his agitation would not subside. I was mistaken, however, in believing that I was the object of that anxiety.

"And what did Luigi say to you?" he asked suddenly, and I was stunned by the passion with which he had absorbed that name and my initial words—"Luigi sends you his best"—working them up into such a stark and anguished preoccupation. He had always appeared to share with the rest of the city a mild contempt for the old Marxist, even if they saw each other frequently and their wives were friends. Luigi refused to recognize in Rea any other quality than that of being amusing. I realized at that moment how much, instead, Rea respected Luigi. I didn't answer right away. Cora was serving the spaghetti and he said, "Enough," after two forkfuls. He didn't eat much, like all those who are ambitious. He knew that eating put one to sleep.

"So what did Luigi say to you?" he asked softly.

And when I pretended to be distracted, he said: "I'd really like to know."

And before I could answer, he said: "He detests me? Tell me the truth. He detests me, doesn't he?"

I heard the sound of his fork flung down angrily on the table. It was as if all of a sudden the ceiling had opened and from that stagnant sky snakes rained down among the dishes. We continued to eat, heads down, until Pratolini ventured: "Why should he detest you?"

"He doesn't detest you in the least," I said.

"You want to make me lose Anita's friendship, too!" Cora complained. "As if my life mattered anyway!" and she burst into bitter tears, with her head on the table.

"Idiot," Rea said. "Any minute now I'm going to slap you."

But he made no move, and, lost in thought, he overturned a glass of water.

"Maybe he doesn't detest me, but I certainly annoy him. I'm the most famous writer in Naples, but that's not my fault. I've always been nice to him. I don't think he amounts to much, it's true, and actually I despise him, but he knows that. The truth is that I'm healthy and he's sick. Healthy as a writer, I mean. I love the people. I, in fact, am the people. My mother was a *vammana*, a midwife, that's for sure, the truest truth. As for me, I was a worker, then a peddler in Brazil, and finally a writer. Down there, for example, I wrote articles for *Fôlha da Mana*, an important newspaper. I've had many jobs, now I'm a writer. But not a writer like so many others. I studied the classics. Boccaccio, Manzoni are my gods. I have a library and the books are nothing to laugh at. I don't laugh. I grow, live, expand. I'm ambitious, of course. This house is only the beginning. But I also think of others. I want everyone to have a house like this, and a bathroom, and a telephone. That's why I follow closely what happens with the Party, and the Party follows me. We understand each other. We are against leprosy and cancer. We are for science applied to nature, yes, we are. This is the secret. Luigi, on the other hand, what does he want? He wants to laugh, all he does is laugh. I spit on a man like that."

"Yes, all he does is laugh," Pratolini said guardedly. And then, after some hesitation, he added, "He's finished."

"Don't you think so?" Rea asked.

"You don't just leave the Party without an explanation," Pratolini said. "Something about that man is evidently no longer functional. I understand someone who never joined (though I think it's a limitation), but I condemn someone who leaves."

"So you agree?" Rea asked.

"I think we shouldn't talk about it anymore," Pratolini said, and he turned to look at the fish that Cora was placing before us. "This is one of the most wonderful things about Naples. In Rome you can't get it."

Rea, instead, refused the fish and began to eat an apple, but soon threw it away.

"It's rotten!" he said, turning to Cora. "Bring the coffee to the study."

The room appeared to be the smallest but also the most beautiful in the whole apartment. The entire wall on the right was taken up by ceiling-high bookshelves made of a pale wood and packed with vividly colored books, almost all of them brand-new. In front of the bookshelves, and made of the same wood, was a large desk, more suited to a draftsman than to a writer. Between the bookshelves and the desk was a chair. On the desk, which had practically nothing on it, was a huge lamp. Another lamp, painted yellow, in the shape of an elongated funnel, hung from a nearby beam. The wastepaper basket was made of brightly colored straw and also seemed brand-new. On the floor in a corner was the typewriter, along with a lot of books that had not yet found a place. On the opposite side of the room there was a small couch, two wicker chairs, and a low table. Through the window in the central wall I could see reinforced-concrete apartment blocks under a shrouded and blinding sky.

Rea stopped on the threshold and cast an attentive and passionate eye over all those things, then went to sit at his desk. Pratolini and I sat in the chairs, while Cora remained in the doorway, regarding her husband rancorously, with her usual tormented expression of a beloved and wounded pet, as if she were about to burst into tears. Then, almost without our noticing, she slipped out of the room.

I felt that Rea was still upset by our conversation at the table, and I wanted to distract him by revealing to him the real reason for my visit—the interview for the illustrated weekly magazine. I had thought he would be pleased by the prospect, but instead he heard the news with indifference. Perhaps he had no faith in my abilities as a journalist, or it annoyed him, as often happens with men from the South, to see a woman involved in such things. Whatever the case, he demonstrated not the slightest interest.

"Oh, yes?" he said distractedly, and turned to Pratolini. "You should see it when it's done," he said, indicating the room with a sweep of his hand, "not now. Here there will be a rug. That couch and those chairs will be replaced. I already have in mind certain paintings for the walls. Tell me the truth, do you think Crisconio* is any good?"

"I don't know his work ... or very little," Pratolini said vaguely.

"They've promised to give me one as a present."

"In that case, you have nothing to lose," the writer responded.

I had been staring at Pratolini for a few moments, and I don't know why, but it seemed to me that in spite of his smile he was vaguely disillusioned, unhappy. He had come to Naples, perhaps on business, but above all out of the need to return felt by those who have once been on these streets, feeling themselves exiles in any other place, under the illusion that they would

---

* Luigi Crisconio (1893-1946) is considered by some to be the most important Neapolitan painter of the 20th century and has been compared to Cézanne. He had limited success in his lifetime, often selling his paintings for little money to the middle class.

hear or see something extraordinary, the air of Olympus, in this wretched city. But instead he found nothing here, no one was waiting for him, his friend was paying him little attention, and many other such things must have been weighing on his heart. Perhaps, without his even noticing, the bullying humanity, the sorrows of the people bothered him, and, forced by his beliefs to seek out some friends and not others, he was asking himself if he hadn't made a mistake in asking Rea to have a friendly chat.

"My book is being translated everywhere, including America and England," he said, turning to me with that meek, slightly sad smile of a neglected child, and hoping that Rea would pay attention to him, but Rea was once again lost in thought. "But who knows how well it will do in any case."

"Why shouldn't it?" I asked.

Pratolini was about to respond when Rea interrupted him. And as if he had been thinking of nothing else, he asked me, in an almost threatening tone, "And will you also write about Luigi?"

I tried to ignore the question by pretending not to have heard it.

"I'm speaking to you!" Rea shouted, hitting the desk with a pencil in irritation.

"Oh, I don't know, I don't think so."

"But it's important. Negative, of course, but important. Naples of yesterday. You can certainly compare him to me."

Cora reappeared with the coffee, and suddenly the young man became wildly cheerful. His small pockmarked face lit up like the stones of Naples, when, in the night sky, fireworks explode, first in silence, and then with whistles and loud bangs.

He stood up and ran to embrace Cora, nearly knocking over the coffee cups the surprised and unhappy girl had just managed to place on the low table. He spun her around rapidly, pressing her to him, while from his lips came a torrent of words, at once fervent, daring, vain, foolish, and infantile, and even the dullest of them sparkled. Cora squirmed and finally got free of him.

"Go and change your shirt," she said forlornly, "because at three we're going to see Anita."

"I love her very much," he said, once the girl had gone. "She's a fiery woman. Her problem is that she's always crying. Sometimes I tell her: You should have had a bourgeois husband, the kind that makes love only on Sunday." And he laughed some more in his arrogant, happy fashion.

In the meantime, neither Vasco nor I had dared to say a word. Far from forming any opinion, we were continually overwhelmed by astonishment, as if the young man before us were not a citizen but a force of nature, a nature that was epileptic and perpetually astonishing. More than Naples, where that force is by now weakness and hysteria, he was Campania, a product of those furious peasants and carters who press at the gates of Naples—the happy land where thought can't escape from the confines of sex, from tumult and the weight of blood. In a flash he was someone else, out of control, blessed. And yet he wasn't a fool. Even his violence and his vanity were terrifyingly serious. As he had indicated, he didn't know how to laugh. His vision of life did not extend beyond the mechanical contortions of the people. He was able to describe these things perfectly, if with detachment, since he himself was a detached and ancient son of nature. If he had not been proud of this ancientness of his, he would have been simply ancient and inconceivable. But he was, of course, proud of it, he knew he was ancient, and this conscious pride was enough to strip his writing of all truth, thereby causing a split in his creative world. And so it was that the most active and truest side of himself lay in his gloom, his lust, his incessant suspicion and incessant fear of Luigi's judgment, not in his capacity as a man of letters but as a man and a mirror, even if blurred, of that nugget of conscience that had taken hold in Naples just after the war.

He drained his cup in one gulp. "Tell the truth, you're not a fan of the real people!" he said to me abruptly, sitting down next to me. He had resumed that calm demeanor that I was familiar with, wary and a bit tough.

Right then, I had no idea how to respond.

"You were scandalized a moment ago when I embraced my wife. Among your kind, these things aren't done. You're hypocrites."

Again, Vasco and I didn't breathe a word.

"Aren't I right?" he asked, turning toward Vasco.

"You're right, only we weren't scandalized in the least," Vasco said. "We simply watched."

"And you found something to criticize, I suppose?"

"Nothing," Vasco said.

"Nothing," I said.

He smiled. Then some extraordinary thought occurred to him and, no longer attending to Vasco but looking at me furtively, he began to take off his shoes, peering at me to see if this act of his would disturb me. He wore cotton socks, of the same blue as his trousers, and yellow at the tips of the toes.

"Do you like these socks?"

I asked how much they cost and he became irritated again. "You said you wanted to interview me, and you still haven't asked me a single question. Go on, write."

He grabbed the lined notebook I had put on the table and quick as lightning placed it on my knees. In the meantime, he continued to peer at me to see if I was looking at his socks. And he swung his foot right under my nose so that I would see it. I didn't know what to ask and sat there awkwardly, eyes lowered, confusion in my face. Seeing me thus and interpreting my situation as some kind of feminine dismay, he was overcome by pity as well as worried about the integrity of the interview, and tearing from my hands the notebook he had given me minutes earlier, he opened it and began to write himself with great and meticulous attention, and a kind of peasant's calm. He had to put his feet back on the ground, of course, but he was already absorbed by his most profound passion, the cultivation of his own fame, and had forgotten about that little whim. When Cora reappeared, wearing a hat (a black derby with two shiny green feathers and a veil), he gave me back the notebook with a brilliant look that was full of professional understanding, and I softened toward him. I glanced at the notebook. Beneath a page full of notes on his work, along with the names of critics who had praised him, there was a number: 200774.

"What's that?" I asked.

"Don't you see? It's written underneath," he said, looking at Vasco with a strange smile in his eyes. "It's my worker identification number."

Vasco didn't say anything, nor did Cora, nor did I. And Rea, after a while, though he did not sigh, turned gloomy again.

A few moments later he left to get dressed to go out, and I saw that even the light in the clouds had dimmed.

"WHAT IS THE MEANING
OF THIS NIGHT?"

~⌒~⌒~

"Prisco and La Capria," I said to myself later, with my face pressed up against the window of the bus, as I watched the street in Arenella recede. And with those names I sought, almost mechanically, to distract myself, to emerge from the oppressive state of lucidity and fear provoked by the sight of uninhabited places, silent herds, a weakened sun over a static landscape.

It thundered for a long time, in a hidden place in the sky, but didn't rain; in fact, the sky that had seemed turbulent and about to burst with water slowly cleared, and on the gray sea framed by the bus window, like a silver snake behind the dull green vegetable gardens, the islands reappeared.

Remembering Prisco and La Capria, whom I knew well, was like seeing them, and I already knew how they would receive me if I went to visit them and what they would say. The former had found himself a place on Via Crispi, one of the most aristocratic streets in Naples, after winning the Venice Prize, I believe. Once, I had been outside his house and I remembered very well that small, four-story white-and-orange building with large terraces, colorful shutters, and windowsills decorated with pots of flowers. He was a very calm young man, a little chubby, refined. The names of his characters—Reginaldo, Delfino, Radiana, Bernardo, Iris—were perfectly literary and had nothing to do with our region. They were a sign of his isolation and, even more, of the serene detachment of his imagination from the furious and ever grim reality of this land. He was lovely to see and listen to, but was of a time when truth was not what was sought. I couldn't say the same of La Capria. By now everyone had heard of his book,* and I, too, had read it. Much as there is of the intricate and murky, the hybrid and fragile in that story full of references to Proust and Moravia, and so unable to be itself, it successfully portrayed the place on this earth—Naples—in which nature had confronted certain European experiences, but had been unable to suppress them, and remained stagnant, while her citizens half-heartedly protested and complained in the growing darkness. I saw again the young man's home in Posillipo, in the grottoes of Palazzo Donn'Anna; I envisioned the light-blue-and-white sweaters he wore—until a few years back he'd been one of the neighborhood's sought-after youths, always bored and barefoot on the shore. Despite all this, I wasn't convinced that he could

---

* La Capria's first novel, *Un giorno d'impazienza* (*A Day of Impatience*) was published by Bompiani in 1952.

be identified with Naples, and, in fact, he was not Naples but the culture and vices and virtues of a southern bourgeoisie that always ends up settling in Rome. Instead, I was looking for something that was Naples, Vesuvius and the counter-Vesuvius, the mystery and the hatred of the mystery, the terrors of the child of these streets, of the devotee of these streets, who was suffocated by them, or stopped being suffocated by them, only to return to being suffocated by them.

As the bus teetered along Via Giacinto Gigante, threatening at any moment to tip over, as if it were drunk, I had the sensation that from the windows of one of those buildings I was being stared at by a fair-haired man with two proud and childish eyes, while his beautiful hand rested enchanted on the pages of a book. But this had to be a mistake, because Gianni Gaedkens, one of the most renowned members of the *Sud* group—the other being Luigi—had long since left Naples to try to find work in Milan. I couldn't have seen him, and I told myself that I had been hallucinating.

"I'll go find out," I thought, "I'll go ask Prunas about him." And so I remembered him also, and thought about meeting him—I hadn't seen him in a very long time—before I left Naples again.

Still wobbling and plunging, the bus had in the meantime reached the great red walls of the National Museum. It crossed the piazza named for Dante at a pace that had become normal, even tired, and continued on Via Roma. It stopped three or four times. At one of these stops I got off.

I found myself in front of the Bank of Italy, a little before the Augusteo Theater, in the part of the street that goes from the huge building housing the bank to Piazza Trieste e Trento, passing the Galleria Umberto and Vico Rotto San Carlo on the way. Here ended (or began) the famous Via Roma, once called Via Toledo, named for the Viceroy Don Pedro who opened the road in 1536 over the western moat of the Aragonese wall. Almost completely straight, on a slow incline from south to north, two kilometers and two hundred and fifty meters long, as the guidebooks claim, it is the main artery of the city. Stendhal defined it as "the most cheerful and most populated street in the universe," and I suppose its fame still resonates.

Much like the previous evening in Chiaia, although it wasn't yet the same hour, here, too, there was a great commotion, a feeling of extraordinary excitement, as if something had happened—a murder, a wedding, a victory, two horses breaking loose, a vision—but then drawing nearer I saw it was nothing. The faceless throng filled up that marvelous street and poured in from the surrounding alleys and looked out all the windows, mingling with the bourgeois crowd the way a dark, fetid water, gushing out of a hole in the ground, would pour, swelling, over a terrace decorated with flowers. There was no acknowledgment of the presence of these lower classes on the faces of the bourgeoisie, but it was still a terrible thing. It wasn't just two or three old mothers, the kind who scratch their heads, dragging a lame foot, their big eyes dulled by memories—there were a hundred, two hundred. There weren't five or six men with concave chests and shifty eyes, their hands crossed over their chests, but at least a thousand. And if you had been looking for just one of those putrid girls who adorn the windows of the narrow streets with their yellow faces, grimly singing and laughing in hushed tones, you would have been abundantly satisfied. The promenade was full of them. If then you had a desire to find one of those boys between five and ten years old—who, when the U.S. Navy is in port, traffic in tobacco and their sisters with the Americans— because you wanted to ask him to do something or simply look him straight in the eye, you would have been terrified by the sheer numbers. In fact, the streets were paved with their gray flesh. And in the face of this, how wonderful and strange the serenity of the bourgeoisie appeared! I told myself that two things must have happened a long time ago: either the people had, like the volcano, opened up and vomited forth these more refined people, who, just like something *natural*, cannot see something else that is *natural*; or this category of humans, which was, by the way, rather limited, had, in order to save themselves, renounced the ability to see the common people as living beings who were a part of themselves. Perhaps neither of these forces, born of nature, ever considered the possibility of revolt against its holy laws.

When I reached Via Santa Brigida, I heard the sweetest voice calling my name, and, looking up at a five- or six-story building, I spied, in the distance, on a top-floor balcony, the ecstatic face of a young man who was awkwardly looking out: it was Franco Grassi, one of the two sons of the dean of Neapolitan journalists, Ernesto; Franco, too, was an editor at a local newspaper.

"Wait a minute, I'm coming down!" he called to me.

Looking around, I understood why Grassi had been looking out. Something had actually happened here. The front door of one of the buildings was only half closed and from one of those balconies came loud weeping. Many people, both working class and bourgeois, were silently forming a circle on the sidewalk beneath that balcony. They appeared to be attentively looking at something with quiet eagerness and, moving closer, I saw on the ground a bright red stain surrounded by other, smaller stains, like red leaves scattered around a red bush. Some, especially the children, stuck out a foot in order to touch it. I learned, almost without having to ask, that half an hour earlier an eighteen-year-old housemaid had thrown herself from the third floor after an argument with her employer. Word was going around that the woman had previously been arrested for maltreating her employees, but the building's custodian, an enormous gray woman, who was coming toward us with a pail, denied that. The employer had nothing to do with the situation. Giovannina Alatri, the name of the deceased, had a few hours earlier given herself a cold-wave permanent, against the will of her fiancé, a certain Ciro Esposito, a swindler. Having learned what she had done, this fellow called her on the phone to break off their engagement. At first the young woman laughed, then she threw herself off the balcony. Almost certainly she didn't want to die; she only wanted to *make an impression* on him, but she broke her neck: while she was dying she had yelled, "Help me!" A red-faced old woman on the second floor who had been listening to all this shouted that that wasn't true, either: she knew Giovannina Alatri, and she was certain that she would never have done such a thing, because she was a pious girl. The guilty party was the government, which had exiled the royal family. Ever since then, Giovannina had changed; she no longer slept at night and was always invoking the king. Giovannina had recounted to her the dream she had had that very night: "The sea will *turn upside down*, the mountain will split apart and burst into flames, and the sky will turn into ashes above this ungrateful city."

"Shame on you!" shouted a voice from a nearby balcony. "You still support the monarchy, even after it betrayed the Duce!"

There was the sound of glass breaking, then a great commotion, and laughter.

I turned and saw Franco Grassi, who was coming toward me from the opposite sidewalk. He was small and frail, just as I remembered him, and he rocked slightly as he walked, thinking of very sweet things. His eyes were green, and his forest-thick black hair swallowed up his thin face. He was very elegant and was sucking on a finger as he looked at me, like a child.

"I've almost finished the first part of my novel," he said, extending his small, tired hand, "but I don't like it much anymore. You, how are you? What are you looking at?" he added, in surprise.

I was looking at the main door: the crowd had parted to let two women come out of the building. The head of one was covered by a shawl, and a dark old hand clutching it was all that could be seen of her. She was shouting in a voice that didn't seem to be her normal one, full of anger, as if somehow the horizon she was seeing were not the same clear, delicately colored one that we saw, as if, in fact, she weren't seeing anything human anymore, but was dragging herself through some kind of crypt, as she screamed in dialect:

"*Pecché nun fa juorno? Che vo' di' sta nuttata?* Why isn't it daytime? What is the meaning of this night?"

"Mamma, calm down, in his infinite bounty God wished to punish us," the younger woman sobbed.

They got into a dilapidated taxi waiting at the street corner, perhaps for the first time in their lives. The young woman was, perhaps, showing off, while the older woman for a moment showed her face in the window, red, as if she were drunk and spellbound. In the pervasive light that was becoming tinged with azure and pink, the taxi pulled away and no one spoke anymore, and, little by little, with odd smiles, the crowd dispersed.

Near me, Franco had watched all of it, his eyes clear and alert.

"What no longer convinces me," he said after a moment, "is talk that is too grandiose. Pride betrays us sometimes, especially when it comes to autobiography. May I offer you a coffee?"

Walking next to him, I knew that his indifference was a form of control. Everyone was indifferent here, everyone who wished to survive. To become emotional would be like falling asleep in the snow. Guided by its most delicate instinct, the bourgeoisie never stopped smiling, and, continually jostled by the common people, by their painful sorrows, by their madness, resisted patiently, like a wall lapped by the sea. It was impossible to know how long this resistance would last. Ultimately, even the bourgeoisie had its troubles, and these troubles were the impossibility of believing that humankind was different from nature, and they had to accept nature in all its amplitude; these troubles were the age-old habit of respecting nature's orders, accepting from it the enlightenment as well as the horror. Whereas among the working class every so often a revolt would erupt and over the high prison walls would come curses and the sound of laments, here, among the bourgeoisie, reason kept an absolute silence, afraid of upsetting with even a minimal observation the equilibrium in which it still endured, of seeing its days melt away in the sun as never before. This fear, a fear stronger than all other sentiments, kept a stranglehold on all of them, and prevented them from voicing any simple truths, any human rights, and, in fact, from uttering in its true meaning the word *man*. Man was tolerated in these parts by invasive nature, but only on condition that he acknowledge himself, like the lava, the waves, as part of it. From Portici to Cuma, volcanoes are scattered about this area, they surround this city, and the islands themselves are ancient volcanoes. The clear, sweet beauty of the hills and sky was idyllic and pleasing only in appearance. Everything here smelled of death, everything was profoundly decayed and dead, and fear, only fear, accompanied the crowds from Posillipo to Chiaia.

Passing Vico Rotto San Carlo, now called Piazzetta Matilde Serao, we caught sight of two or three people in front of the Bar Leda. One of them was the old soul Orio Bordiga, the son of Amadeo, the former leader of the Italian communists. He'd gotten fat, but was still as adorable and absentminded as he'd been at the time of the Fascist University Group; his large head, with thinning hair, was bowed slightly over his chest, and he wasn't really looking around. I knew that some time earlier he had founded the Society of Authors Without Publishers, and it was likely that things hadn't moved forward at full throttle. Things of the past must every so often have come to mind, as his chin kept sinking farther toward his chest. The car and pedestrian traffic (it was the hour when many journalists were coming out of the building opposite, where several newspapers had their offices) did not distract him, and he didn't even seem to notice what was happening directly under his nose. Almost in the middle of the piazzetta, with a coffee cup in one hand and a few pieces of paper in the other, Vittorio Viviani, with his innocent faun's head, was cheerfully reading out loud the first part of his unpublished novel, which tells the story of a nun's love affair. The person listening to him was not young Orio but the Leda waiter. Carrying a tray loaded with coffee cups that he was supposed to be taking to the various editorial offices of *Mattino*, *Corriere di Napoli*, and *Unità*, he was mesmerized, and the coffeepot was swaying.

Seated on the sill of a *Mattino* window, one of the editors, with a brown, half-naked chest revealed by his open shirt, was slowly eating seeds, quiet and absorbed, and spitting the shells down onto the pavement. From the door to the offices of *Il Mattino*, directly beneath that window, emerged a pale, thin young man, wearing eyeglasses and a nice smile on his lips. He stopped, evidently distracted, to look at the time, and in that moment I recognized him. It was Renzo Lapiccirella, one of Naples's purest Marxists. For some years, because of cold and hunger, he had scarcely spoken, but his eyes were clear and stared off into the distance, like those of a dying Christian. A large car stopped next to the sidewalk and a gigantic, well-dressed man got out. This was Giovanni Ansaldo, the editor of *Il Mattino*. He quickly headed for the door to the newspaper's offices, while with one finger he brushed some ash off the lapel of his jacket, and, as he passed, Lapiccirella, silently, like the statue of an angel on a tomb, moved aside. The editor above continued to spit seeds.

Everything was so vivid, and those various characters, in a scene that might have been described as serene, were so somber in their precariousness, their melancholy, their solitary remarks, their sighs—so perfect—that for a moment I was tempted to look for the director of this exquisite work; and though I didn't see him, and told myself that he didn't exist, and that this was not a set but one of the many hallucinatory moments of Naples, I felt uneasy at the thought of going in. It was as if the normal air of the world did not circulate in that alley, and those crumbling walls, that gray, and the strange pinks and the greens could, if touched, vanish. I said to Franco that if he preferred we could get a coffee at the Caffè Gambrinus.

"The coffee's the same," he said, "or maybe a little darker."

This café is at the intersection of Piazza Trieste e Trento and the tortuous Via Chiaia. I had spent many hours there during my Neapolitan nights and I remembered it as very large and smoky and full of mirrors. Now even the windows seemed smaller to me.

Just as when you are coming out of a dream you often fall into another one, and the barely wakened brain darkens again, and, inside, an invisible hand turns on myriad lights, I saw people who had filled the pages of postwar Naples, I saw them again but without the joyous postwar halo, in the mists of a summer evening.

THE BOY FROM MONTE DI DIO

The head of the group was the son of Colonel Prunas. He wore a cotton shirt and blue linen trousers. His shoes were black and small as a girl's, as were his dark hands, and in fact everything about this minute person suggested an adolescent rather than a man. An unfashionable watch, held on by a faded strap, gleamed on his wrist. Pale eyeglasses cast a shadow on his downward-tilting face, which was thin and quiet, of a brownish yellow. Only his lips were animated by an imperceptible smile, full of hostility; the rest of his face remained impassive. He was so still he seemed dead, dead on his feet. Instead he was listening.

Next to him, taller and thinner, slightly hunched, and leafing through some pages, stood the man I believed I'd glimpsed at a window on Via Giacinto Gigante. He must have left Milan some time ago. He was no longer dressed in yellow, as he was when I knew him, which was the style of those intellectuals who, coming from an impoverished bourgeoisie, in the first years after the war renewed their wardrobes at the market stalls selling secondhand Allied goods. Those years hadn't been wasted. Black, tight-fitting trousers hugged his long, thin legs; a white silk shirt covered his arms and his hollow chest. On his chin he had grown a blond goatee, which accentuated the expression on his face and in his eyes, at once ecstatic, discouraged, and greedy. His head moved this way and that, resembling in particular two things: a dying eagle and a flower. He had the same bloodless ferocity, and the grace. In one hand he held a very neat pile of papers covered with large, confused handwriting, in the other a cigarette. A coffee cup, empty, sat on the counter in front of him.

A short distance away from these two young men, and staring at them vaguely, with a sharp yet melancholy eye, was a man still young, tall, with a narrow, wan face, who was talking affably, breaking off every so often for a brief yawn. This was Nino Sansone, the editor of the Neapolitan edition of *Unità*. He didn't seem to want to be there, in that company, but he wasn't disgusted, either; rather, he seemed calmly resigned. All around, American sailors were coming and going, like wild white birds in their close-fitting shirts. The glass doors opened and closed continually to let these young people through as they came up from the port, full that day of pale steel ships.

The first to notice me was Gaedkens, who stopped reading and said slowly, "Oh!" Prunas reflexively took note and turned toward me with an expression of both surprise and fear. His faint smile grew, then suddenly vanished from his silent face.

Franco had walked in ahead of me saying these simple words:

"She has come back and she says hello."

"Good, how are you?" Gaedkens said. "We're very well."

In this frankness, which was exaggerated, more like impudence, and in the extreme calm and the smile of one who will never be surprised by anything again, or suffer or rejoice, except mechanically, I recognized him. And I recognized him also in something strong, like a burst of anger, a dream, or weariness, which was ignited somewhere deep in his eyes as he looked at me.

I shook this and that hand, and I had to notice that all of them were dry and a little cold, not sweating like Luigi's, or burning like Rea's. Right afterward, Prunas took off his glasses and cleaned them with his shirt, a habitual gesture especially when he was anxious. His eyes seemed huge, black, intent, slightly reddened by fatigue, and without light.

"Two coffees," Franco ordered, leaning heavily, wearily, on the counter. And turning to Nino he said, "A woman threw herself off a balcony half an hour ago, and I have to run and write it up."

"Yeah, I heard about it," the young man responded with a small yawn, "while I was passing by Santa Brigida. She died instantly."

"Here they're always killing themselves the same way," Gaedkens said ironically. "The balcony. The balconies and the windows of our city don't seem to have any other function."

Prunas didn't breathe a word.

"I see you've returned to Naples," I said to Gaedkens. "I thought you were in Milan."

I threw out these words in the hope that they might stir things up. For some moments I had been feeling the same chilling sensation as when I stopped to contemplate Vico Rotto: that everything was thought, imagined, dreamed, and even realized artistically, but not true—a disturbing performance.

"Not exactly to Naples but to the South. I live in Ostia, and on Saturdays I come back to see Vesuvius." Laughing, he explained, "As you might imagine, Vesuvius is just an expression. I mean I stay in touch with old friends."

Who these friends were, there was no doubt: one of them was there, his pale face alert.

I felt that I was being examined with a terrible intensity, and I discovered behind his eyeglasses, which Prunas had put on again, sorrow and infinite curiosity. "You must have pity," said those dull eyes. "You must try not to look. Is it true that we are dead?" he asked. "Is it true that we've been absorbed by the city and now are at peace?" Perhaps I was wrong, because the young man then contradicted that lament by saying in a hard and rapid voice: "We seem provincial to you, I imagine."

"Absolutely," I was about to respond, but I was upset. The leftist young man yawned again. It was only a tic, but it gave his thin face an expression of detachment and boredom, while instead his entire brain was hard at work.

"I won't go to Milan because my work is here," he said, "but I don't understand those who find work in Milan, then leave that city to come back to the South. Oh, and I'm not referring to the economic advantages, but Milan is enchanting, especially in the winter, with all that fog. A real Stendhalian city."

"We can agree on that," Gaedkens admitted.

Franco handed me my coffee, whose dark liquid had by then dripped into the two cups.

"When I'm tired," Nino continued, "I often dream of spending the winter in Milan. I'd hole up in a cheap hotel on the outskirts and for entire days I'd sit and watch the fog from my window. I was once in Normandy: peaceful, and the sound of the sea as if only imagined. Fog, for me, renews these sensations of stillness and life at the same time."

As he spoke, his eyes became blacker and gentler, his face lowered, another small yawn twisted his mouth, and without saying more the editor of the leftist daily paper went off.

"Amusing," Gaedkens said as we were leaving.

His lips were smiling, but his eyes had become thoughtful.

We set off as a group, without speaking, on Via Chiaia, embedded between Monte di Dio, which is reached by an elevator, and the sloping terraces of the Vomero. We didn't know where we were headed and had no intention of going anywhere in particular. But once on the streets of Naples, you can't help moving in this direction and then that, without any purpose. Usually, when you reach Naples, the earth loses a fair measure of gravitational force and you no longer have weight or direction. You walk aimlessly, you talk for no reason, you're silent without motive, etc. You come, you go. You're here or there, it doesn't matter where. It's as if everyone had lost the capacity for logic, and were navigating in the profound and complete abstraction of pure imagination. I did notice one thing on my left, where the young Prunas was walking: and this thing was a sorrow so concrete, so enormous in its silence, as to constitute the only counterweight possible to the sweet anarchy of the earth. For only a few minutes, since the brief conversation at Gambrinus, that sorrow had become conscience, lucidity, violence. Reason's friend hated me, because of the memories I brought back in him, because of the mirror I held up to him, a concave mirror, in which his youth was deformed. And it was also strange that, beneath that kind of death, that vague decadence of skin, glances, words, I could still feel the steady beat of life. The young man of another time, alive in that death, was thinking.

And here is the dialogue that unfolded while we were walking, including Franco, who had forgotten about the urgency of his article:

PRUNAS: We, too, are amusing, I imagine.

ME: No, not really.

PRUNAS: That's even worse, naturally.

GAEDKENS: Luckily, nothing offends us. That's the only advantage of Naples.

FRANCO: And then, anything you think, we've already thought it.

PRUNAS: So, tell us the truth.

I remembered the many times Rea had besieged me with this curious sort of interrogation and I said to Prunas that I was struck at that moment to find that he had the same peculiar obsession as Rea. I knew that this observation would wound him. In fact, I saw him lower his face and smile one of his brief, sad smiles. But a moment later he had raised his head again. And I noticed something I had observed before, something that had always surprised me: there was in that mind the power of a wild beast, of unbroken generations, incapable of conceiving the word death. In Naples, the Sardinian youth had immersed himself in misery, but he hadn't died; he was old but not yet dead, because he was unable to conceive of the word death. He was incapable of emotion, of being sad, except at moments, and they were soon forgotten. His thirst for life, his capacity to build a life, were both suffocated and immense. And still in my imagination appeared the figure of a harsh and indomitable beast. With a hard smile, he asked:

"And how is Rea? I imagine you've seen him."

"Yes, I saw him."

"And you must have seen Luigi, and Incoronato, and La Capria."

"Luigi, yes. But not Incoronato and La Capria, and not Michele. Only Pratolini."

"And Pratolini was content, I imagine."

"Yes ... but not entirely."

"Because of Rea, I imagine."

"Or because of Naples, which is the same thing," I said, "and I can't say he's wrong."

"Why?" asked Prunas. "Naples isn't good enough for you?"

"No," I replied, "this silence isn't good enough for me."

"Why, isn't everybody speaking?" Prunas said cheerfully. "Where is this silence that so impresses you? Have you ever seen a more loquacious city?"

"No, I truly haven't seen such a city, but I haven't seen one so silent, either."

While we were walking, our configuration was this: Prunas and I were ahead, Gaedkens and Franco behind. Gaedkens was speaking, he was speaking yet his voice resembled silence. It was the voice of someone who loved form, exquisite and therefore remote, not the voice of a man but the echo. Franco responded in monosyllables, sometimes he didn't even respond at all, and I heard behind those monosyllables, or silences, the full conversation. Prunas had not objected at all to my words, but had simply lowered his head again.

I remembered that somewhere around where we were there had once been a cinema club. After Prunas closed the journal, he couldn't rest until he found something else to do, and he had come to an agreement, yet again, with the sad men of *Voce*, now *Unità*. So, little by little, he took over the cinema club and brought to the theater on Via dei Mille, among many other films, *The Battleship Potemkin*. It had been an incredible morning, the theater packed with shocked faces, profoundly wounded by something. They didn't speak, but they absorbed everything: the fierce nakedness, the courage, the music evoked by the scenes. Upon leaving, and for days afterward, they had all met at Sant'Orsola, a small room full of books, between Palazzo Cellamare and the Chiaia bridge, that had once been a library. It was springtime and the sky over Naples had the same color as any sky in Europe where men stroll. Many hopes were born that day, strange hopes between wakefulness and sleep, and I had seen Renzo Lapiccirella and the other men from *Unità* smile as they spoke congenially with the young writers from *Sud*. We had arrived at the same place between the noble palace and the bridge, in front of the gates of Sant'Orsola. The gates were open and the door to the room at the end of a small courtyard was also open.

"Shall we go in?" I said, and while I said it, I asked myself if we had really stopped in front of Sant'Orsola, or if we weren't mistaken and it was one or two doors away.

Neither Prunas, nor Franco, nor Gaedkens responded. They seemed embarrassed, while the colonel's son looked inside indifferently, unmoved.

I looked, too, and this is what I saw:

The little room where young people had once gathered was dimly lit, not as before when many lamps had cast a white light. In place of the table there was now a small counter, and seated behind a sort of cash register was a dark-haired, bearded woman with big, languid eyes under a surly brow, selling tickets. A few thin, mesmerized people were standing before the counter staring at a sign on which was written: "Entrance 150 Lire." Some were looking at the sign, some at a dark curtain hiding a door to another room. From the other side of that door came a silence, and a particularly cold draft, as if there were snakes lying back there. Some went in, others came out, men and women, all poor, on their faces an abnormal excitement. At a certain point, behind the curtain, which remained open for an instant, something clear sparkled, and in that thing—a simple glass coffin—one could see a long form. It was a man in black, smiling, who looked around patiently, smoking a cigarette.

I wasn't sure if I was on Via Chiaia or in a distant, exotic city, or in Paris, perhaps. I wondered if I had had a drink of something strong while wandering anxiously around Naples. I heard and didn't hear Franco's words.

"That's a fakir," the editor of *Giornale* said to me. "He's been fasting for several weeks already."

"At the cinema club?" I asked.

"It's no longer the cinema club."

"Why not?"

"We didn't pay," said Gaedkens ironically.

"Neapolitans," Franco said kindly, "rightly prefer these shows to others. They are more relaxing. They are, ultimately, contemplation and repentance, in other words, Naples."

I looked at Prunas, and he seemed even smaller than he had earlier—more than small, shrunken, like those Indian heads that some Brazilian tribes reduced to the size of an orange. He didn't smile or move an eyelash, imperturbable. And I wondered if he was extremely alive or only extremely dead.

I calculated the time that passed in this way: the sky was

no longer pink, but purple, and evening had descended. We all remained immobile in front of that gate, looking across the lighted courtyard at the low building of Sant'Orsola. We looked at the sign just as the public did, as if considering the possibility of buying a ticket. In the end, I asked the young man whose wan smile I glimpsed beside me, asked him gently, what exactly he was doing in Naples.

There was no answer to this question.

"But do you work?" I repeated. "Or at least are you thinking of working?"

The wan smile beside me became slightly more attenuated before disappearing. The young man blew his nose indifferently.

In that abrupt blowing of his nose into a very clean handkerchief, there was some childish embarrassment, and some stubbornness. And I said again:

"Are you hoping for something?"

It was as if I were talking to a wall standing in a plain inhabited only by the wind.

So I was certain that he was truly dead, finished. He was stubborn and lost, although at first glance he didn't seem to be. None of those whom I had met so far had hidden from me his death. I had seen the declaration of the end, of failure written in fairly clear characters on each face, like an eviction notice on a shabby door: behind it one could glimpse a fire that was about to go out, a bent back, terrified eyes; or even a fire that is wildly blazing but will go out. Here on this stony face nothing was written. Even the ironic quips, the flashes of brilliance, the restless smiles didn't reveal his internal reasoning, said nothing of what was happening inside him. They were intended more to deflect attention than to attract it. My conviction of a little earlier, that the energy of our companion was inexhaustible and his hope indomitable, was due to the agitating effect of the coffee and had vanished. The person I saw at my side among the other silent youths was a little man with a withered face and a dull stare. He was someone who no longer had the courage to raise his eyes, to resume a conversation, to think clear and logical thoughts. The city had destroyed him. And why shouldn't it have destroyed him? They had all fallen here, those who had wanted to think or act, all talk had become confused and only augmented the painful human vegetation. This nature could no longer tolerate human reason, and, confronted with man, it rallied its armies of clouds, of enchantments, so that he would be dazed and overwhelmed. And this young man, too, had fallen.

This was what I was thinking, irritated and sad, and now, behind me, Gaedkens seemed to confirm my doubts, with his vague and monotonous accent, even vaguer from moment to moment, as if his imagination were torn. Speaking of Naples as a phenomenal terrain, he delighted in the transience of the land, which was continuously changing shape, where nothing was stable and everything generated deception and fear. "In place of this fakir," he said, explaining urbanely to the young Grassi, "it's very likely that tomorrow we'll see a castle. Here where we see the putrid Chiaia, this very night the sea may take its place, and there where you see Vesuvius, tomorrow the Greeks may reappear, with their families and their games. The laurel, like nothing, could be transformed into a pine tree." Hadn't we seen the purest of the Marxists look around with their eyes wide open, and others mutter their desire for fog? And all the young writers I had known, were they not singing the praises of their ancient mother? Was there even one who would cast the light of human reason on nature? All, all of them were sleeping now near the sea, they were sleeping from Torre del Greco to Cuma.

"And so?" Prunas asked abruptly, but calmly.

"And so, nothing," Gaedkens said, smiling. "You can call out for centuries and no one will answer."

A lively and incredulous smile once again lit up Prunas's face, a totally inadequate response to Gaedkens's words, something that still surprises me to think of. But he said not a word more.

We left the gates in front of Sant'Orsola and started walking again until we reached Via Filangieri, where the previous evening I had watched Guido cool himself with a woman's fan, and speak with such anguish about Luigi. Luigi was suddenly in front of us, lame, but still tall and handsome, his delicate head obscured by a mask, through which his blue eyes were visible. We saw him right there, under the clock tower, with his wife and son. He was walking slowly, slightly hunched, his face forward as if he were looking for something. We all saw him, but it was pure imagination. At that hour Luigi, in his lonely apartment, was staring at the glass door to see who went by in the street, or greeting a friend with a smirk.

We also saw La Capria: he was leaning lazily on a friend, turning his graceful profile, his eyes incredibly bitter. He greeted us with a gesture, but we knew that this was pure imagination. Maybe in Rome at this hour he was bent over a desk at the radio.

A little later, we saw others: Vasco was walking with Incoronato, while Rea, dragging along the bewildered Cora, searched for Luigi in the crowd. Michele Prisco, who had no suspicion of wonder or terror, was engaged in a pleasant conversation with some women.

All, all of them, were before our eyes: the scattered youths of *Sud*, the tired men of *Voce*, and with them returned the jumble of useless days, windy, with a mixture of sun and rain, perfectly useless, except for the fact that they had left the trace of this anxiety.

At this point, Prunas left us and ran ahead along Via Filangieri, as if he had seen someone or something that interested him. I wanted to know who or what he had seen, and so I, too, pulled away from the others (and didn't see them again later; they went home) and joined him. His old face remained pale and hard, just as in the best days of his adolescence. He didn't speak to me, and I said nothing to him. We walked for a while together along Via dei Mille, which was strangely deserted, passing by the Caffè Moccia, where Cardillo, in the same position as the evening before, was watching Slingher and Capriolo, who continued to hold forth on Neapolitan dialect, and Vincenzo Montefusco was still sitting at a small empty table, turning his neck every so often, on account of his tic. We kept going, and I remembered that he was always like this, in the years of *Sud*, when he was on his way to the printer: taking these small rapid steps without seeing anything, cold, his thoughts intent on what needed to be done. I seemed to understand with immense wonder that he had neither imagination nor emotion, at least not in the normal sense, or if he did he considered them a kind of energy that had to be continuously controlled, and this allowed him not to be afraid of Naples. Like all monstrosities, Naples had no effect on people who were barely human, and its boundless charms could leave no trace on a cold heart.

And so I took up the conversation of a little while ago. Perhaps, on his own, the young man would respond.

"What do you think you'll do now?" I asked him again politely, as if time had not passed.

The curt response was:

"Nothing."

"What do you mean, nothing?" I persisted.

"Nothing, unless I have money, I meant."

"And if you had money?"

"Machines, a print shop."

"Anyone can get machines," I said, "if they have the money."

"They wouldn't be just any machines," he said coldly.

"What kind of machines would yours be?"

"Free machines."

"Aren't machines only machines?" I quietly objected.

"There are machines and machines," he answered. "Machines that are made by humans and machines that *are given* to humans. The ones that cure them are the former."

"You mean they must be made in Naples, not imported? Is that what you mean?"

"Certainly."

"But you don't have money for anything, it seems to me."

"Not a penny."

"And so?"

"And so, nothing."

"Some years have already passed," I said gravely, "many have grown old, maybe you've also noticed. A couple of wrinkles, a tic that's become more pronounced, seems like nothing."

He winced at these words, then seemed to become indifferent again. "It's not possible that nothing ever happens. One day, perhaps, something will happen. Then I'll be happy I stayed here to wait for it."

"And if nothing happens?"

He didn't answer. Once again, like a stubborn child, he blew his nose, in order not to answer me.

I didn't know if I was sorry for him or if I admired him. He was so small and obstinate. Soon Naples would suffocate him as well in its vast embrace. He was like a red ant on the slope of the mountain: it couldn't see or couldn't tolerate that terrible majesty; it sped along, lightly and insensitively, thinking that it would build its defenses here, its fortresses.

"Are you going home now?" I asked, seeing that he had stopped.

"Yes, I'm dog-tired."

He barely smiled as he shook my hand, then he turned back. I stood watching him for a bit, until I couldn't see him anymore. Quick as he was, he must have already reached Monte di Dio.

Then I went back to my hotel, and as I thought about the many fates of the many people the night passed, and dawn appeared, on the day I had to leave. I went to the window of that building that was as tall as a tower and looked over Naples: in the immense light, delicate as that of a seashell, from the green hills of the Vomero and Capodimonte to the dark promontory of Posillipo, all was united in sleep, a marvel without consciousness. I also looked toward the red walls of Monte di Dio, where the young man from Sardinia, so simple and cold, was perhaps at this hour still thinking, shut up in his dusty room, and I don't know what I felt. Only the calm wash of the sea over the rocks could be heard, only the hills could be seen, increasingly vivid and victorious in the light, and, farther down, the buildings and gray alleys, the miserable, diseased alleys, where among the piles of garbage some lights still shone. But the day was rising ever higher and more brilliant, and gradually even those last lights went out.

AFTERWORD
The Gray Jackets of Monte di Dio

⁓ ⤳ ⤳ ⤳

T he promoters of the "*Gruppo Sud*" exhibition asked me some months ago to write this note.

It seems right to me to end the new edition of my book with it, as evidence of how the young Naples of that long-ago postwar period, as represented by the *Gruppo Sud*, was at the origin of *Chronicles*—was impetus, inspiration, and a constant support in the realization of my project. Finally, the idea—that emerged in these pages—of the *intolerability* of reality, an idea I had never considered before, has made my vexation with describing humans and things more comprehensible. Now everything is peaceful in the south, but if the flag of utopia still waves, at least in my heart, it is because of the Gray Jackets of Monte di Dio.

I'm afraid that I never actually saw Naples, or reality in general. I'm afraid that I never really knew Italy either before or after the war. What allowed me to juxtapose these things, and talk about them in some of my books, was the emotions, along with the sounds and the lights, and even the sense of cold and of nothingness, which came from those realities. In sum, I did not love the *real*; for me it was almost intolerable, even if I didn't really know it. Where this intolerability came from I still am unable to say, or I would have to look into metaphysics. But it was with this lack of consciousness of the real that, in the thirties, I wrote my first stories, and after the war the others. In the first stories there were lights, sounds, emotions, and, in the background, the anguish of an inconceivable—because of his horror and grace— Edgar Allan Poe, whose uncanny pages I had first encountered. In my second book of stories, on the other hand, reality—the abnormal reality of Naples at the time—was there; but, to tell the truth, it wasn't *my* reality, I hadn't sought it out. Pasquale Prunas was there beside me to point things out and tell me about them actually and historically.

What I still remember about the postwar period is not the Palazzo dei Granili, or Vicolo della Cupa, or the miracle-filled streets of Forcella; what I remember is the street, or neighborhood, called Monte di Dio and the Nunziatella Military Academy, and the house of the noble family from Cagliari who lived there, the family of Colonel Oliviero Prunas, the headmaster of the academy.

So, the Nunziatella, its courtyards (or was there only one?), its severe buildings, the silence, the order in that military school, and, by contrast, the irrepressible energy and vitality of the young Prunas and his friends, and the generosity and warmth of his family and their friends—all remain part of my authentic memory of Naples. Emotions, lights, and sounds, then: not a measure of the grave reality of Naples and the world that was waiting outside.

I couldn't accept that reality: I had already glimpsed it and pushed it away elsewhere. But it so happened that Prunas's journal, the bimonthly of commentary on current events conceived by him and longed for by him and his friends, that very modern and extreme *Sud*—extreme and in its way revolutionary—needed to document this "reality." Pasquale Prunas was convinced that I, too, would be able to do that; and in order to stay longer, without too much compunction, in the enchanted shadow of the Nunziatella, I went in search of documentation. It was my testimony of the underbelly of Naples, where I had spent my adolescence; thus I recalled and compared it with the "historical" Naples that we now all have before us, and I wrote a good part, or at least made a complete outline, of my book on Naples. It was, therefore, a *vision* of the intolerable, and not a true measure of things (I was, and still am, incapable of taking the measure of things), and this choice was the result of a decision, which I remember with gratitude, made by the journal's editor.

I say "editor" in order to soften my tone of voice. In reality, he was the boss, the commander of a small band of ambitious, serious, educated, obviously poor young people who constantly gathered around him. They came from the working class as well as the middle class, and were distinguished by the religion of knowledge, of books, of information, and also by modesty of dress, the common habit of wearing the gray jacket—thus that small group, adopting as its uniform, which was also ideological, or perhaps revolutionary, the mild gray jacket, not the red or blue of the new Italian divisions, that group obeyed him to the letter. And so I, too, obeyed, choosing between measure and vision, I, too, preferring vision. And that was *Neapolitan Chronicles*.

And afterward? Afterward, it was time to leave. We left (or died?), one by one, all of us. Pasquale Prunas stayed on. And it's not difficult for me to hear the echo of those hesitant footsteps that led me, and then the others, along the peaceful sidewalks of Monte di Dio to stand before the large door of the Nunziatella, closed at that hour, on the last evening hosted by the First Gray Jacket.

And I can see the small, dismissive, and sweet smile on his handsome face and imagine how he went on remembering the happy years of his and our eruption (of renewal and joy), not thinking that they would end; and how suddenly, not hearing our footsteps anymore, he looked around and understood that, yes, all was over. I can imagine the gentle shock of it. Perhaps he looked up for a moment; perhaps his pace slowed. Perhaps it was an evening no longer cold, and very calm. He thought of staying on. The courtyard was there, empty and silent. All the goodbyes had already been said. But why imagine so much? He had decided. So he turned his back on the courtyard and began to descend without sadness toward the city.

ANNA MARIA ORTESE (1914-1998) is one of the most celebrated and original Italian writers of the 20th century. *Neapolitan Chronicles* brought her widespread acclaim in her native country when it was first published in 1953 and won the prestigious Premio Viareggio.

ANN GOLDSTEIN has translated *The Neapolitan Novels* and other works by Elena Ferrante, as well as writings by Primo Levi, Giacomo Leopardi and Pier Paolo Pasolini. She is the former head of the copy department at *The New Yorker*.

JENNY MCPHEE has translated works by Giacomo Leopardi, Primo Levi, Natalia Ginzburg, Paolo Maurensig and Pope John Paul II.